The Canyon Cuts Both Ways

HIDDEN STORIES

Cover Photo by Alden Rodgers
Cover Design by Heather John
Crow illustrations by Kurt Hollomon

Cox, Dan T.
The Canyon Cuts Both Ways/ hidden stories
978-0-578-62618-5

1. FICTION / Short Stories. 2. FICTION / Small Town & Rural. 3. FICTION / Family Life, Marriage, and Divorce.

This is a work of fiction. Names, characters, places, organizations, and incidents either are the product of the author's imagination or are used fictionally, and any resemblance to actual persons, living or dead, events, or locales is entirely coincidental.

Printed in the U.S.A.
Distributed by Ingram

The Canyon Cuts Both Ways

HIDDEN STORIES

Dan T. Cox

The Canyon Cuts Both Ways

For my daughters, Shannon and Erin

Ah listen, for silence is not lonely!
Imitate the magnificent trees
That speak no word of their rapture, but only
Breathe largely the luminous breeze.

—D.H. Lawrence, from his poem, "Corot"

Prologue

An east wind sometimes blows down this forested canyon: morning air escaping over the Cascade Mountains, rushing from the high pressure over Central Oregon to the lower pressure due west, descending unremembered slopes, gaining velocity as it fingers along the bottoms of lonely ravines and forgotten draws, slipping over the flatness of reservoirs and then cascading over the spillways to the churn at the bottom, and then farther on in flow with the North Santiam River, crowded at every bend and set of rapids by legions of looming, breathing evergreens.

It is a clean and purposeful wind, stout and pure. One that erodes most troubles and makes many things seem briefly possible, or at least more palatable, or sometimes just comprehensible.

Mostly, this wind clarifies the promise of each day it blows; speaking plainly to anyone willing to listen and learn its truth: that if you get up and go out into it, if you shake off your apprehensions in favor your aspirations, even if only for a short while, then you will be far better off than if you don't.

Canyon dwellers, those who know this particular east wind, can tend to regard it as proprietary and selective—a kind of personal possession. You have to live in or frequent the right spots, though, or you miss out entirely. If you're too far upstream or downstream all you may sense is a mere breath of airflow bordering on inertia.

To embrace it best, you have to be somewhere along that stretch of river that flows from the base of Big Cliff Dam toward the rocky narrows of Niagara, where the North Santiam resisted long-ago efforts to dam it with chunks of chiseled stone and Chinese labor. This is where the canyon sucks in tight and the river constricts into a threatening mood. This is where the winds compress, and become even more resolute.

Now, there are far too many days when no such wind arrives. Its oddly recuperative properties are missed in ways as random and unique as the people who call the canyon home, and who count on this gusty affirmation. Some can start to privately lose their bearings if too many of those windless, blasé days string together. People can go slack without realizing as much, and then they forget to look up toward what remains of a hopeful sky, devoured and reduced as it is by canyon walls and trees grown tall.

That's when the canyon forces things.

That's when you have to decide whether that subtle, encircled sense you get from being there is more like a reassuring hug, or a disquieting restraint.

The canyon cuts both ways.

PART ONE

King Bean

Green pole beans came ready in August. Retired yellow school buses pulled up to the edges of fields at daybreak with sleepy-eyed pickers. They were kids from up the North Santiam Canyon who were old enough to work but too young for jobs of distinction. Country kids doing fieldwork. United by their dislike for bean picking. Motivated by their need to earn money for the state fair and new school clothes. Kids like the Sawyer boys.

Virgil was the older brother at fourteen. Sam was two years younger. Virgil was an overweight, pimple-faced, slow-witted disappointment to their parents. Sam was exactly the opposite. The only thing they did well together was fight. And though Virgil's size often allowed him the advantage of simply sitting on his little brother, it was Sam who typically inflicted more damage. Because of the things he'd say.

They were collected each dark morning at the end of their driveway by a bus that no longer had the authority of flashing red lights. They went each day with sack lunches and frozen cans of pop insulated with newspaper. They sat apart on the bus. Yet they shared a reluctance to leave the warmth and drowsy rhythm of the bus for the stiffening chill of the fields.

With a five-gallon bucket in one hand and a dirty brown burlap sack in the other, Virgil and Sam trudged with the others behind the row boss—an unremarkable middle school math teacher named Mary Soderberg who also needed summer money—following her along the dirt road that circled the field to the section due for picking.

The numbered rows were assigned at random to pairs of pickers, one for each side of the tall wall of vines. Gunnysacks were dropped to the ground, where they'd wait to be filled by the bucketful. And then came the sound of those first few beans hitting the bottoms of metal buckets. Firm green beans bouncing off of thin, cold metal, echoing upward out of the empty buckets like crude megaphones. Proof to humorless Mary that someone was actually working. Virgil and Sam worked near each other, but not together.

Long sleeves were necessary when the picking day began, because the unfriendly green vines were wet and cold from overnight irrigation or heavy dew. There was no way to keep arms dry or hands warm. The only option for most kids was to pick hard and wait for the arrival of direct sunlight.

For the Sawyer boys and a few mischievous friends, however, there were better things to do. Like smoking stolen cigarettes. Or reaching through the vines to steal beans from the buckets of more industrious pickers. Or throwing beans at girls in an all-out effort to target their breasts. Anything to avoid picking. But the favorite distraction of all was a competition called King Bean.

The idea was to find a large, overripe bean that had grown into the shape of a horseshoe. The bean was held in one hand by forming a fist and inserting the ends of the bean on either side of the middle finger, snug into the webbing at the base of the fingers. Before all this, though, the bean had to be looped through the horseshoe shape of the opponent's bean. With the battling beans interlocked, it became a simple tug-o-war. One bean broke. One didn't. The winner was the King.

Sam had a knack for picking winners. Virgil did not.

And so it happened that on the morning of the last day of the picking season, Sam had a bean that defeated all challengers.

He was delirious with self-congratulatory excess—whooping and hollering and aping through the rows like a crazed court jester, completely unaware or unconcerned that he'd become an irritant to everyone within earshot. Especially to Virgil, who'd long since given up hope of ever finding a King Bean, and who deeply resented his brother's grandstanding.

Then Virgil saw it. The bean. The potential heir to the throne. Hanging right there on the vine. Right in front of him. The perfect u-shaped bean. Ready for battle.

Virgil picked the bean carefully, and marched through the rows toward his loud-mouthed brother.

"Well whadaya know," said Sam in a voice for all to hear. "Looks like Fat Boy wants to play. Whadaya say, Fat Boy? Wanna take on the King? Ya wanna try, Lard Ass? Because I gotta warn ya. I'm invincible. And you're gonna get screwed, blued, and tattooed. So ya better not try if you're not—."

"C'mon," said Virgil abruptly.

With that, the Sawyer brothers faced one another there among the pole beans and the pickers and the buckets and the gunnysacks. They each presented their beans with methodical, ritualistic motions. Sam's bean was in position first, directly in front of Virgil's chest, held loosely in Sam's untightened fist. Virgil lifted his hands toward Sam's fist, preparing to loop his challenger behind the defending champion.

But just as his hands neared his brother, Virgil hesitated. A look of confidence washed over his face. And then, with uncharacteristic speed, he snatched Sam's bean away and instantly stuffed it into his own mouth. Virgil smiled as he chewed Sam's bean into oblivion.

The King was dead.

Stunned by his brother's coup, Sam's eyes filled with tears. Then anger. Then he launched himself into Virgil's legs, low and hard. And with that, the brothers fought what they would later refer to as their famous bean field fight, the one that somehow changed their relationship for the better.

Meanwhile, Mary Soderberg leaned against the fender of the dirty yellow school bus in the morning sun. She listened to the commotion caused by the Sawyer boys as if it was distant music, drew deliberately on a slender cigarette, and revisited the grinding regret flowing from a particular memory: that sweaty summer evening three years prior when she closed down the Narrows Tavern with Russ Sawyer, the boys' father, and then went with him into the shadows of the lonely parking lot to do something that helped neither her marriage nor her standing in the canyon.

The Mill City Bridge

I never told anyone this story before because it felt embarrassing to have been so shallow. If I tell it poorly now, let's just chalk it up to a lack of practice.

My name is Vincent Mays. I was a child most of the 1960s. My immediate family had people coming of age during three different decades, because I had four brothers and three sisters. This was not at all unique for my hometown, Mill City, Oregon—one of those towns where a percentage of people grew up wondering what the hell they were doing there and how long it would take to get out. Nothing original in that, though, right?

I grew up in love with cars. Distracted by them, really. Priding myself in an ever-increasing knowledge of years, makes, and models that was always at my disposal.

Secondary to this was my belief that the front grillwork of cars often resembled facial expressions. More often than not, people tended to drive vehicles with expressions that matched their own. That's how it was with the 1960 Thunderbird coupe driven by Johnny McCall, Mill City's preeminent hood.

Coming toward me from the opposite side of the green steel bridge that gave our town a splash of architectural character, Johnny's car was threatening. Between the pavement and the Thunderbird emblem was a low-slung grill; an elliptical open mouth with a lazy lower lip, unwilling to either smile or purse as it gulped in air to feed the radiator. The twin headlights were small and close, like eyes looking forward with intensity but seeing nothing of interest. And immediately above the headlights, cold eyebrows of Detroit steel. Bodywork that sent shivers. Angry metal meant to intimidate. Low and mean. Furrowed in perpetual displeasure. Creased with angst. Sharpened like a blade by the air splitting off the leading edge as Johnny McCall cruised the hapless evening streets.

The baby blue exterior did nothing to lessen his menacing forward motion. The fact that Johnny McCall could look so frightening in a soft pastel color merely stood as a Turtle Waxed testimonial to his brand of bad. Driving a black car would have been far too easy.

Of course, he was a high school drop out. Of course, his future was bleak. And of course, the United States Marine Corps looked forward to putting his disagreeable nature to good use at summer's end. But none of that really mattered as Johnny McCall came at me on the bridge.

What mattered was a much simpler thing. It was a question. One that would be answered in the time it took the grumbling Thunderbird to cross the bridge, which for a few moments on a warm August evening served as an inadvertent meeting place for an unevolved 14-year-old and a calculating villain on the road to no where good. And yet it was not a question that necessarily needed to be answered just then, because I was patient for my age and willing to wait.

Drawing nearer, the personality of the car gave way to the persona at the wheel. A skinny 18-year-old in a white t-shirt, with a bright white cigarette secured behind his driver's side ear, in vivid contrast to his dark brown hair.

That was some head of hair. Although short on the sides, it was otherwise tall. Almost erect. He combed it straight up from his flat, vertical forehead, without a part, and then straight back over the top. It was all held in place by who knows what; some sort of ointment that passed for hair dressing, which he had reportedly pilfered on a regular basis from the basement of a mortuary somewhere. That's what people said anyway.

His teeth were Easter white. And straight. And except for the slight gap between his two front teeth, they seemed perfect. But rather than frame them in a smile, he showcased his good-boy teeth in a slightly opened-mouth grimace that allowed him to smoke the cigarettes he transferred from behind his left ear. It was a wonder either ear could actually hold a cigarette, because they were small and trim, and they swept back sleekly against the side of his narrow head, like window wings, always postured for high velocities. Johnny McCall looked fast, even as he idled.

There had been many stories and rumors about Johnny McCall. About his crimes. About his dangerous older friends from out of town. About his father in the penitentiary. About his ability to procure beer and marijuana. And perhaps most impressive of all, about his knack for distracting good girls from their paths of virtue.

Most guys his age despised Johnny McCall. A few feared him. Especially the good guys. The athletes. The brains. The leaders. So they worked hard at ignoring him, but their girlfriends could not.

I was not yet old enough to be part of this resistance effort. And though I was certain not to follow in the tire tracks of a troublesome soul like Johnny McCall, I sensed the vitality of his danger. I knew that for one reason or another, he seemed just a little more alive than most. Maybe it was because he also seemed a little less likely to live out his life. Whatever it was, in my eyes he had standing.

Steel bridge parts obscured my initial view of the Thunderbird. In the homogenous, desaturated light that happens just after a summer sunset, the luminous baby blue flashed brightly between the gray-green girders of the superstructure. The closer it got, the more I could see of the car. Then Johnny himself.

Instantly, he was beside me on the bridge.

We'd never spoken. He'd never acknowledged me. I had no reason to expect anything of him.

Our eyes locked.

Johnny McCall sneered, flicking his head back with the same abruptness and blasé efficiency he used to dispatch ashes from his cigarettes.

Then it happened: without giving me even a second to prepare, Johnny McCall answered the question that I had not intended to ask but apparently had asked by simply looking him straight in the eye and not looking away.

He flipped me off. Casually.

Gave me the bird.

The finger.

Me.

Vincent Mays.

Now try to appreciate, under normal circumstances this would have been the ultimate gesture of rejection. Complete and utter condemnation. Outright dismissal. A public embarrassment, and a vulgar insult as well.

But that's not how it was. Not at all.

Because in that town, on that evening, at that twilight moment, reclining in the driver's seat of that Thunderbird, encountering me between the gray-green girders of that bridge, Johnny McCall meant to send a different message.

It was an endorsement. An evil blessing. A letter of recommendation signed in his own hand. It was an unmistakable signal that the coast was clear. And that as far as he was concerned, all was well with regard to my standing in the social order of things in that crucible of a canyon town. His passage on that bridge became a passage of life for me. From that point forward—if I chose to be—I was in.

Vincent was in.

What a wonderful feeling. What a revelation to one minute be shuffling along in my Chuck Taylor high-tops over the coarse concrete of the bridge's sidewalk, and the next minute be walking on air, having been anointed by the best possible bad guy in town. My ego swelled with each step. My confidence soared.

It was as if I'd come face-to-face with Lee Marvin as Liberty Valance, fearing for my life, but then unexpectedly being judged worthy of continuing to live it.

That 1960 Thunderbird had six round taillights. Three on each side. Enormous tail lights, which flashed like railroad crossing signals when Johnny McCall tapped lightly on the brakes to slow for rough, uneven pavement at the end of the bridge. And with that he was gone, save for the subsonic rumble of his twin glass-pack mufflers, which I could hear long after he was out of sight.

I was grateful to Johnny McCall. My view of Johnny and his friends was sympathetic and supportive for several days after that watershed moment on the green steel bridge. This, even though he never actually acknowledged me again. Nor did we ever actually speak to one another.

So it followed that the elixir of Johnny McCall's blessing wore off. And in no time I came to hold him in the same disregard as the athletes and brains and leaders who I'd intended to best. In fact, I squandered the opportunity to be bad before Labor Day, opting instead to one day drive a car with a more pleasant expression.

Johnny McCall never made it to the Marines. On the Sunday afternoon of that Labor Day Weekend, his baby blue Thunderbird somehow managed to plant a kiss on the massive chrome bumper of a loaded log truck that should not have been out on the highway on a holiday. He died at the scene with his Thunderbird.

It turned out to have been appropriate that my allegiance to Johnny McCall died young. Because I learned a few years later, while home from college on Christmas break, that I had not come to his attention on my own merits.

I had not come by my social standing honestly. Indeed, I had been the beneficiary of unsolicited help from a family member.

The truth was revealed to me on Christmas Eve by my oldest brother. Confused by rum and Coke as to whether I had previously been told, he brought up the topic amid the retelling of several shopworn stories, meaning my brother attached no importance to this little gem.

It was my middle sister.

She was the one who had been embraced by Johnny McCall that summer. She actually rode in that Thunderbird. She talked to Johnny. Hung out with him. Partied, too. You know the rest....

All these years, and I've never quite been able to discuss Johnny McCall with my sister, let alone tell her how grateful I am to her for his validation. But I've always sensed she knows as much.

No Bears Out Tonight

The Potter brothers were silent as they drove through the blustery March night, down the graveled back road to Don Bewley's house. At nineteen, Rib was three years older, many pounds of muscle larger, a good bit homelier, and a few car-lengths smarter. He drove. Pretty brother Jim rode shotgun.

On the seat between them in Rib's bronze 1958 Buick Special were the things they required: cotton pillowcase, electric cattle prod, roll of narrow masking tape, white string on a spool, and this logging town oddity: four sections of an old car tire borrowed from the front steps of Simm's Grocery that were cut down to shoe length—two pair of crude galoshes—meant for loggers to slip over their spiked boots to protect the weary wooden floors of the grocery store.

They encountered no one on the back road, which was what they hoped for. Yet Jim was nervous about being seen. Rib was not, because their father had instilled a crafty confidence about not getting caught at or even suspected of the practical things the Potters did to make ends meet. Things like spotlighting deer after dark, raiding rural mailboxes, poaching deer out of season, stealing cedar from the National Forest, and taking tools from truck shops. Easy stuff.

Jim was still in training, though there was some question as to whether the lessons were sinking in.

This was a nervy first for them, and risky enough that only Rib and Jim could ever know about it. Even Rib felt concern about whether they'd find the final item they needed there at Don Bewley's.

Rib pulled off the gravel road just around the corner from the house Don Bewley rented, off into the brushy darkness of a short dead-end among the tall firs. The knobby jumble of large, round river rock in the roadbed kept the car from making tracks.

Opening their doors as Rib silenced the motor, the sounds of that night came in on the brothers. A gusting wind blew through the black treetops, making a constant, homogenous sound similar to distant ocean waves. To their right, occasional traffic from up on the highway joined in; tires on pavement and contoured steel displacing heavy night air. The sound the brothers were most heartened to hear, though, came from the river. It whitewatered to their left, at the other edge of the woods, deep at the base of a sheer drop-off that ran right behind the house. The top of the embankment was Don Bewley's unfenced backyard.

They did not speak.

Rib gestured to Jim that he should stow the tape and prod and string and pillowcase inside the sections of tire, each loosely laced with a shoestring tangle of red electrician's wire. They did not latch the car doors. Carrying their crude tire overshoes, they stayed on the river rocks to get back up to the gravel road. They stepped high and clean to hush their approach. The packed gravel of the driveway simplified their path to the kitchen door in the breezeway between the little white house and its detached one-car garage.

Don Bewley taught high school and claimed to be a weekend mountain climber. He was part way through his third year there in the rural canyon school district, which hired him to teach Spanish, Social Studies, and Modern Problems. He stood six feet five inches tall but lacked the athletic build to go with the sport he professed. The opposite of chiseled. But he made up for his physical shortcomings by being intellectually fit, intelligent to a fault, witty, glib, sarcastic.

These qualities drew people in. Drew students inappropriately close to him. Younger, weaker male students, whose trust he fueled with an easy manner, and with the "chin up" feeling that came from getting a quick, confidence-building snug around the shoulders from his enveloping right arm.

That was the modern problem being addressed on this particular night; the unforgivable way he betrayed boys—particularly Jim, at heart a good boy who loathed disappointing anyone.

He lived alone. Rib did not personally know Don Bewley, because he graduated before the tall teacher's arrival. Rib had seen him around a lot, though, driving that navy blue Sunbeam Alpine and looking ridiculous with his round, balding head protruding above the windshield.

A ceiling fixture lit the kitchen. Dirty yellow incandescence leaked out through the window in the kitchen door, through the screen door. It defined the breezeway and threw a pale glow through a third door that opened to the garage, to the blue Alpine. He was home, somewhere inside.

Rib and Jim stopped short of the main garage door, still on gravel. They removed the stuff from the sections of tire. Rib put on his temporary overshoes and then slipped into the garage, beside the Alpine and out of the light. He found what they needed—climber's rope—hanging there on a spike in a stud of the unfinished wall. Rib retreated to the rear of the Alpine with the flaccid coils of rope looped over his head and one shoulder. He gestured Jim to come in with the other stuff, which Rib took from him in preparation for the next step.

Jim remained tense but contained. Focused. He knew what to do, because his big brother had coached him through it repeatedly. He stepped up to the kitchen door and knocked.

A few tight-chested moments passed, then the door opened.

"Hey, Jimmy!" said Bewley as he opened the door, his round face smiling. "Didn't expect to see *you* tonight."

"Yeah, it's me," said Jim, faking a tone of resignation, the screen door still between them.

"Yes, it's you. The promising young canyon man who's lucky to find me here at all. Ya know, you really should've called first."

"Just to be sure?"

"That's right, Jimmy. Just like we've discussed, because you know how these imbeciles around here like to talk."

"Uh-huh," said Jim, as he looked down at his feet and then back up into Don Bewley's small eyes, understanding that this ruse depended on his ability to behave just as he had on previous arrivals at Bewley's backdoor.

"Listen, I was just about to throw on a Jiffy Pop. Maybe have a beer. Watch a little TV on the couch…."

The smiling teacher finished the thought by gesturing with a quick head movement that Jim should step inside.

Say no this time.

That's what Rib had drilled into him.

Stall him.

"I dunno," said Jim as he took a step back.

"Hey, what's the matter?" said Bewley with false sympathy. "Jimmy Potter's feeling a little shy tonight?"

Jim did not reply, but the thought flashed through his mind that what he felt wasn't shyness. Cleverness, maybe. Or family pride, here to ease the nagging shame that he and a half dozen other boys came to know at the hands of Uncle Don. Certainly righteous revenge sparked by outrageous betrayal. But not shyness. Not now. He took another step back.

"Well," said Bewley. "You're obviously uncomfortable, which makes one question why you even bothered to show up at all."

"You want I should go?" said Jim, now in the center of the breezeway and still drifting back. "Maybe I should go."

"No, Jimbo. Don't go," pleaded Bewley as he put pressure on the screen. "Not after you went to all the bother of getting over here."

Jim spun on his heels and moved toward the darkness of the backyard. Toward the river.

Hem and haw.

"I dunno know, Mr. Bewley. I feel all mixed up."

"It's Uncle Don. And if you're not sure about things anymore, I really think we should sit down and talk. Sort it out together. Like before."

Bewley stepped out the kitchen door in response to Jim's discomfort. The screen door squeaked with unsavory tension as Bewley surged into the breezeway. His fleshy hands let go of the screen door, freeing the taut coil spring to snap the screen door back against the jamb; a wood-on-wood smack.

In a flash of theatrical timing that stealthy Rib had not foreseen, the pillowcase went over Bewley's head just a beat after the screen door slammed.

Rib wrapped up Bewley in a massive bear hug, using strength and gravity to take the taller man hard to the concrete. The move knocked the wind and the sense out of Bewley.

Jim put on in his rubber overshoes as he went for the gear. The brothers worked together to put a loop of masking tape around Bewley's neck, right over the fabric of the pillowcase, securing the mask without leaving a mark; a temporary attachment. Then Jim tied the end of the string to the top of the pillowcase, working one corner of the bed linen to become the core of knot that would not come undone. That accomplished, the brothers looked briefly at each other for reassurance, but were quickly prompted toward the next step by Bewley's returning awareness, by his pathetic attempts to free himself from the weight and strength and conviction of brothers.

Rib stood him up. It began to rain on the corrugated metal roof of the breezeway, making what had always been for Rib one of the most comforting sounds possible. He took it as a positive sign.

"Wahyooguys...whayooguyswan!?" Bewley tried to say through the pillowcase and his own frenzy. "Wahyoo—"

But before he could complete his excited utterance, Rib sent a crushing fist into the teacher's soft belly. Bewley returned to the concrete, doubled-up, wheezing, trembling. After a few moments, Rib stood him up again. And again, Bewley frantically tried to talk, leaving Rib no choice but to launch an even more menacing blow to the belly. Jim admired his brother's effectiveness.

This sequence repeated until the man with the formal education understood the basic connection between his silence, his pain, and his ability to breathe. This pleased Rib and emboldened Jim, because it meant they could carry on without saying a word to each other or to the lecherous man who had it coming. The brothers energized one another by coolly locking eyes again.

They marched their shrinking giant out into the backyard, where the roar of the river below was more pronounced. They positioned Bewley out in the open, in the dark. Rib held him.

Jim went back for the climbing rope. Then he went to the edge of the embankment and lowered one end of the rope to a point he judged to be about halfway down to the water. Jim laid down the rope in the shaggy lawn, careful to maintain the length that hung over the edge. He stepped past Rib and Bewley as he laid out the rope, moving toward the back of the house. Once he was there, he tied the climbing rope firmly to the wooden legs of the frame that held up a tank of heating oil. Then he walked back to Rib and Bewley and began retrieving the river end of the rope. When it arrived, Jim tied a classic noose and dropped it over the teacher's head. He snugged it on Bewley's neck, below the masking tape and beneath the fabric, rope on flesh.

Rib let loose but didn't let go. He began twirling Bewley where he stood. Making the teacher rotate in his beefy hands, prompting the teacher to continue every time he tried to stop. And every time the teacher tried to talk, Rib plowed another resolute fist into the tall man's soft belly. After several minutes of this, the man was disoriented and defenseless. Rib no longer needed to hold him.

Jim grabbed the end of the white string that ran to the top of the pillowcase. Rib grabbed the electric cattle prod, put it up against the small of Bewley's back and pulled the trigger.

"AWWWW-GAWWWWD!" screamed the teacher as he bolted hard to the left and a few feet from the brothers.

Rib and Jim stayed with him. Another shot of electricity.

"AWWWWWWWWWWW!" yelled the teacher as he shot back to where he'd just been, panting and stooped, whimpering like a sick child.

The brothers followed in their tire galoshes. Rib stood him up and then crushed his fist into the teacher's belly one last time, insuring silence to the end. The prod was applied again and again. Bewley lurched around the darkness of his backyard, trying to divine which way was which. The last zap erased what logic remained in the teacher's brain, replacing it with panic, running him straight toward the river, right over the edge. As he descended toward the rocky rush of water, the string in Jim's hand pulled tight. The masking tape broke away and the pillowcase came off, just before the climbing rope snapped tight, the moment before Bewley's neck broke.

The brothers gathered up their gear and left. Driving back down the gravel road, they finally spoke.

"We gonna get away with this, Rib?" said Jim in a half voice.

"Well sir, it's some mighty big business we took care of tonight," answered Rib as he grinned toward the windshield. "No doubt about it. Good timing on our part with Mom and Dad away for the weekend. And by the way, ain't no need to whisper."

"But is this gonna work?" said Jim in full voice. "We gonna be all right?"

"Oh, hell," said Rib. "We're already all right. 'Cause that flabbyass sonofabitch can't mess with nobody no more. And we're the ones that finally made things right."

"Okay," said Jim, still needing reassurance.

"Listen," said Rib. "Remember that game we used to play when we was younger? There Ain't No Bears Out Tonight?"

"Sure."

"Well, remember how all you smaller kids would go skipping through the yard in the dark, just a chantin' the name of the game together as loud as you could? And how us bigger kids would always be the bears, hiding in the bushes or the trees, waitin' to pounce on you guys?"

"Yeah?"

"And remember how one of you would always get caught?"

"Every single time," said Jim.

"Well, this here's the opposite of that," said Rib. "There really ain't no bears out tonight. And ain't *nobody* gonna get caught, 'cause even though what we done wasn't exactly pleasant, it was damn sure right. And that, little brother, is what's gonna protect us from this night forward."

"Ohhh," said Jim as he put it together, now looking through the windshield like his big brother. "So that's what the old man means by that favorite saying a his."

"You got it."

"Be in the right, and do it at night," said Jim and Rib in unison, using deeper voices to mimic their father.

A few moments passed in familiar silence, then Jim spoke again.

"Ya think the old man would be proud of us?"

"Pro-bly," said Rib. "But Lord knows, we can't never give him the chance."

The brothers returned the loggers' slippers to the front steps of Simm's Grocery without being seen. Once back in their own ramshackle house, they put the roll of string, the masking tape, and their dad's cattle prod back where they got it. They put the pillowcase in the laundry for their mom to absorb into her washday blur. They went to bed in the drafty room they had shared their entire lives; comfortable lying between their sheets, understanding there would be news the next day about that peculiar teacher taking his own life.

"Good night, little brother," whispered Rib.

The Teachings of Anna

"Hey, Uncle Brad," said the seven-year-old boy from the top of the haystack, up near the dusty rafters of the barn. "You know what I think?"

Brad Glover glanced up toward the boy, momentarily taking his eyes off the hypnotic flow of grain pouring from the awkward paper feed sack and into the fifty gallon barrel beside the horse stalls.

"Tell me," said Brad with a puff of mid-winter steam, his eyes back on the grain again.

"Okay, okay, get this," continued the enthusiastic boy. "What if somebody invented a breath freshener for farts?"

"What?"

"You know. Just like a breath mint, only it makes your farts smell better. Wouldn't that be a good idea?"

Brad kept pouring, not wanting to bobble the job and working hard to suppress the chuckle that wanted out. He considered whether young Charlie deserved a reprimand for his topic. But it wasn't a hard call. Not out there in the barn, where nature takes its course. Not with everything the boy had been through.

"Yeah, I suppose you're right, Charlie. That'd probably be a useful thing to have around."

"I know, I know," followed Charlie, who sat down on the highest bale of hay. "We could sell it for forty-nine cents a piece, and we could make enough money to buy my school clothes next year."

"Well, I don't know about that."

Gray afternoon light washed through the open barn doors into the otherwise unlit chamber of hay and feed and dirt floors. The light threw a dull glow right up the front of the haystack, right up to where Charlie's boots dangled. Brad looked up and into the eyes of the boy, who beamed the way he always did when what-iffing in the barn, far from the trouble that steered him into the care of Brad and Randi Glover.

"Got a name for your miracle product?"

"Uncle Brad, I really think we should call it Fart Fresh."

Brad burst into laughter despite all efforts to restrain. Once again, the boy who came to live with the fifty-one-year-old carpenter and his school teacher wife had blasted through the monochromatic humdrum of midlife with wit and charm. Others had robbed the boy of his innocence, yet there remained a magic. A pureness. An undeniable lightning bolt of what is still good in a world that sometimes seems fouled beyond repair.

"Oh, Charlie," said Brad through the trailing gasps of laughter. "You're too much."

"Too much what?"

"Oh, you know. Just too much. It's a figure of speech."

"What's that?"

"What's what?"

"A figure of speech."

"Hmmmm," said Brad as he clanged the metal lid atop the feed barrel. "Well, I guess a figure of speech is one of those things people say without having to think about it. You know? The words just come right out. Kind of automatic."

"You mean like a fart?"

"Yes, I suppose that's about right."

Charlie stayed put on the bale of hay, absorbing a lesson that would surely earn Randi's disapproval. Brad grabbed the metal hay hooks hanging on a nearby post and stepped to the base of the haystack.

"Which one?," asked Brad.

"That one," answered Charlie as he pointed. "I think Jake and Juniper are hungry for that bale of hay."

Brad pretended to inspect the particular bale, kicking it twice, snapping its twine once. Then he shifted his weight onto one leg to ponder the decision further, raising one hand to his chin like a professor lost in thought. He looked up at Charlie, made eye contact again, arched an eyebrow, and pointed toward the bale to confirm Charlie's choice.

"That's the right one. Trust me."

With that, Brad swooped in with his metal talons to impale the ends of the bale and then lift it up onto the fronts of his thighs. He walked the hay a few feet to the horse stalls and dropped it. Jake and Juniper crowded in from the other side, eager to eat.

"Oh! Can I cut the twine this time?" asked Charlie as he launched his skinny body down the front of the haystack. "Can I? Can I?"

"C'mon over here then, but remember what I showed you about being safe."

"Don't worry, Uncle Brad. I'll be careful, because I'm good with knives."

"Nothing less will do," said Brad with authority.

Charlie did the job well, and the bale of hay opened up like an accordion at rest. Brad stooped to grab sections of liberated hay and plopped them into the feeders. Charlie helped, standing on tiptoe to reach the necessary height. Then the man and the boy stood back to watch as Jake and Juniper took over with muscular lips and grinding teeth, blasting equine steam from their nostrils, swishing their tails in celebration.

"Uncle Brad, how come horses don't have last names?"

Brad studied Jake and Juniper as he contemplated the question while simultaneously realizing how much he enjoyed

Charlie's constant barrage of unexpected questions—how proud he was of his nephew's curiosity.

"Now that I think about it, Charlie, these guys do have a last name. It's Glover. Just like mine."

"But nobody ever calls 'em Jake Glover and Juniper Glover. People just call 'em Jake and Juniper."

"Well mostly that's true, except when the vet comes around. He uses their last name in his records."

"Oh."

The screen door slammed shut back at the house. It was Randi stepping out the front door and approaching on the gravel of the barnyard. Brad glanced at his watch without thinking. Charlie stood transfixed by the gnashing horses. The scent of hay and manure and grain lingered all around. Pigeons ruffled up in the highest rafters.

"Potatoes or rice to go with the chicken tonight," asked Randi, leaning around the edge of the barn door.

"Either's good for me," answered Brad in a cheery way that didn't satisfy Randi.

"Well somebody's gotta make a commitment," said Randi with a tone that suggested she'd been through this drill far too many times. "Charlie, how about you?"

The boy thought for a moment, mimicking the hand-on-chin theatrics Brad used a short time before, and then announced his decision.

"I want spanked potatoes, please."

"Spanked potatoes it is, then," said Randi as she made emphatic eye contact with her husband of twenty-seven years. "I'm gonna go check *the mail*."

She disappeared from the barn door. The sound of her boots on the gravel driveway diminished with each step she took, until Brad and Charlie heard only horses again. Both of them felt the late afternoon's first pangs of hunger, but neither spoke of it. Both started thinking about roasted chicken, but then Brad's mind moved on to the chore that remained to be done before they could go in and clean up.

"Charlie, what say we take some firewood up to the house?"

"Oh! Oh! Can I ride in the wheelbarrow before we fill it? Like last time?"

"You bet, kiddo. Once around the barnyard."

"How about three times?" nudged Charlie with a grin.

"Maybe two times," said Brad. "Then it's back to work."

Brad walked over to the pale green wheelbarrow standing on its nose against the wall of the barn. He tilted it down and backed up to where Charlie waited for his ride.

"All aboard," said Brad as he lifted Charlie by the armpits and into the wheelbarrow.

They took off, with Brad trotting in a big circle on the gravel in front of the barn.

"Faster," said Charlie through a giggle. "Faster."

Brad picked up the pace, but not so much that he couldn't glance down the quarter-mile driveway to the mailbox. He saw Randi in her red jacket, motionless, probably reading the most important mail. Maybe a letter from one of their two grown daughters. Maybe something even better.

§

Randi was emotionally stronger than her older sister, Anna. Stronger and wiser. With a far clearer sense of right and wrong, and with an impenetrable set of personal boundaries that sounded like a foreign language to Anna when the topic came up. It was hard for Brad to imagine that they came from the same womb, or that they grew up sleeping in the same room. So damned different they were.

Randi loved her sister. Brad liked her. But neither of them liked being around her or the woe she brought.

The first sign of true trouble came when Brad and Randi's twin daughters were eighteen months old, and there was need for a long-awaited night out. Anna came to baby-sit. The date didn't last that long, because the Glovers admitted over ribeye steaks that the pull of parenthood was too strong. They forked at their temporary freedom, and then passed on dessert.

Randi was the first to notice something didn't look right as they turned in by their mailbox and began up the long driveway in the licorice dark—a peculiar glow. Then Brad saw something in the headlights that didn't belong; a woman's blouse on the gravel. Mint green.

They pulled up into the barnyard to discover a bonfire roaring right in the middle of everything. The liquorous firelight revealed that Anna and the babies were not alone, that others had come. Strangers who danced.

Nobody seemed concerned when Brad and Randi exploded from their car as percussive music blared from the open windows of an unfamiliar car in the dark. Randi ran into the house, past faces she did not recognize, to find the placid little faces of her daughters, asleep in their cribs and unharmed by the chaos. Brad walked toward the music, leaned inside the car, and silenced the radio. Suddenly, the only significant sound was Brad's footsteps in the gravel as he walked among the partiers in search of the largest male. Brad decided it was the tall guy with curly red hair and a clownish smirk; the one who cautioned Brad to back off, even as the father of twin daughters did the opposite. The skirmish was brief and decisive. The man's smirk became something else as he landed on his back, having first been kicked squarely in the testicles and then fisted in the nose.

Randi emerged from the house in time to see beady red taillights driving away into the unsettling night. Everyone was gone but blouseless Anna, who could neither walk or speak. She sat grinning at the flames.

The teachings of Anna were slow to sink in. It took years, and many troubling occurrences, but finally the family understood: the older sister would not easily change her dangerous ways or sharpen her flawed thinking, certainly not so long as she failed to want such changes for herself. It was too easy to go the other way. Too familiar. Too much fun.

Pregnancy did not inspire Anna to change either.

"This bump in my belly," Anna said to Randi one day over zucchini bread and coffee. "It's not what you think. It's not a symbol of my future. It's a symbol of every bad choice I ever made, only this one's got a longer shelf life."

"We're not talking about canned peaches here, ya know," barked Randi in response to her sister's idiocy. "You've got another human being inside you now. You've got responsibilities now. Big ones."

"Listen," said Anna with an inappropriate smile. "There's nothin' new about havin' another human being inside of me. There've been quite a few, and *big ones*, if you catch my drift. Ah for chrissake, Randi, how do ya think I got his way? Don't be so stupid."

Such were the sisterly chats that went nowhere. Such were the worries of the younger one for the older one, and then for the little one on the way.

All Brad and Randi knew about methamphetamines at first was what they heard on the news or read in the paper. But Anna ended up sharing a lesson or two on that subject as well, turning the couple into unwilling experts. Charlie was much younger than seven when the newspaper arrived at the paperbox out on the end of the Glover's driveway; the newspaper with Anna and others on the front page, photographed after their arrest, looking less than human, eyes empty save for their wanton hopelessness.

§

"Hey, Charlie," said Brad as he took another piece of straight-grained alder firewood from the wheelbarrow. "How come you call 'em spanked potatoes? Mashed potatoes, I mean."

The man and the boy stood on opposite sides of the fully loaded wheelbarrow, each doing his part to stack the wood properly in the rack on the front porch. It was a large three-dimensional puzzle, that wood stack, and one they enjoyed working together; finding the best way for each piece to fit into the others, keeping the stack mostly straight, mostly solid, mostly level. It was satisfying, synchronous work.

"I'm sure glad this isn't cedar," said Charlie, sounding older and wiser than his years.

"Because of the splinters?"

"Yeah, I hate getting splinters. Alder has hardly any."

Randi was still down by the mailbox when they first brought the firewood from the shed behind the barn, but Brad noticed she was nearly back to the barnyard and was all but skipping.

"You didn't answer my question about the spanked potatoes, Charlie. What's the story?"

Charlie stopped briefly, put his hands on his hips, and cocked his head sideways for dramatic affect.

"Don't you remember Thanksgiving, Uncle Brad? You were mad about something, and Aunt Randi wanted you to mash the potatoes because you're so strong?"

"I always mash the potatoes," said Brad as Randi drew nearer.

"Well, whatever it was that had you so mad, you kinda took it out on the potatoes."

"I did?"

"You weren't just mashing the potatoes. You were spanking them, and I was just glad you don't get that mad at me."

"Ohhh," said Brad as Randi paused beside him. She had the mail in hand and a grin on her face. She held one open envelope up like a lit candle, flicked it like a deer's ear to focus Brad's attention, and then proceeded on inside the house to get dinner on the table. Brad got the message.

"So that's the story behind spanked potatoes. Huh. Funny how things get their names."

Charlie said nothing further on the subject, choosing instead to bask in the temporary authority a child can feel after solving a mystery for an adult. His little hands reached for the last piece of wood in the wheelbarrow.

"Nice work, Charlie. Sure do appreciate your help."

The look on the boy's face said he liked this chore. Brad's expression was far more complex, because it reflected a wash of competing thoughts: admiration for the boy, a father's love, then a flash memory of the ire he felt for his sister-in-law when she promised to show up for that particular Thanksgiving but didn't—or couldn't—because she decided to capture the holidays with yet another county mug shot.

"Guess we'd better go wash up. But before we do, let me ask you something else, Charlie."

"Okay."

"Well, I was just wondering. How'd you like it if you had the same last name as Jake and Juniper?"

The Unlit Woods

"I can't stand the sound of my dad's breathing," said Paul Walker to the girl he imagined most. "Can't stand to be in the same damn room with him, or in the same car. Know what I mean?"

Yet there he was, riding in the passenger seat of the burgundy VW bus, right next to Lyle Walker and his wind-tunnel nose. That breathing sound rose above the shifting gears and whining engine, masked on occasion by eager questions from twelve-year-old Bill in the back seat. Lyle was taking his boys out for a rainy December deer hunt at dusk.

It was not to be a major endeavor, this hunt, or a pleasant one. Their plan was to take up stands in the densest part of the cold, rain-soaked woods and become part of the slow approach to darkness, waiting for a buck to walk by. This was late season still hunting in the North Santiam Canyon. This was normal for the Walkers.

Bill was old enough to carry a gun, but Lyle was not ready to carry the burden of arming his youngest. Paul was two years older and familiar with the rifle in his hands.

As the three walked away from the VW and toward the fencerow that separated pasture from woods, they agreed that Lyle and Bill would stick close, while disagreeable Paul would go his own way.

"The farther away from him the better," said Paul to the girl again. "Lazy bastard."

The fence marked the western edge of the woods, which meant the remaining light of that dismal, low-clouded day would be no brighter than it was at the moment they parted company. Lyle and Bill went north along the fence. Paul moved south. And when he found what looked like the best spot, he stretched the strands of rusty barbed wire, slipped his lanky frame through the fence, and crept into the woods.

Isolation was a prize for Paul. That it came in the form of hunting made it slightly more valuable. That it began to rain was perfect, because Paul's spirit thrived on the lonely sound of raindrops on dead leaves—the subtle thud of water on that which can only lie there and take it, lightly percussive but without range or resonance. It reassured him somehow, and pleased him as well. Because he let himself believe it was all for him. An entertainment. Like the girl working at the drive-in, with whom he imagined flirty conversations and ambitious compliments.

He wore his first pair of waterproof boots, picked out and purchased by his father as a practical rite of passage. Lyle just stepped into the bedroom shared by Paul and Bill and unceremoniously tossed a large yellow box on the bed.

"Here you go now," said Lyle. "If these fit, put 'em out by the stove to warm 'em up. After supper I'll show you how to grease 'em up to keep 'em dry. Savvy?"

Lyle left the room before Paul could muster any sort of response. The boots fit.

Standing alone in the woods, Paul's feet were home and dry. Sitting was not an option because his jeans would soak through in a second, instantly chilling him to the point of distraction. He was comfortable for the moment, although not fully at ease. And it was in this mindset that Paul became part of the dank woods at dusk.

He tried to care about his reason for being there. But the truth of things came easiest for Paul in settings like this. And the truth of hunting was that he often hoped an animal would not come his way. He'd shoot if necessary. But not to kill. It would be more to hear the roar and feel the kick. And under the right circumstances, when the light was low and the mood was powerful, it would be to see the bright orange fireball erupt from his muzzle. These were his small rewards. But they all paled to the inevitable after-the-hunt chatter with Lyle and Bill about how it went. What he heard. What he saw. How the deer behaved, and whether it was standing still to make it easy or running away to make it hard. Either way, missing was Paul's specialty. Mostly, he wanted Lyle to know that his oldest boy did his damnedest.

As the woods grew darker and the rain picked up, Paul knew that this was when deer moved. He knew that as the light faded and the colors blended, deer felt invisible. He knew that the sound of a million raindrops created an audio cocoon, obscuring the snap of twigs under slender hooves. He knew that because of where he stood and what he could see around him, there was a chance he'd be forced to feign a shot. Yet that knowledge was stowed away in a corner of Paul's mind, present and accounted for, but not on active duty. All he could think about was how mad he was at Lyle. And why.

As the hunter, he was supposed to be silent. But as the angry son, his thoughts erupted into voice.

"You goddamn sonofabitch!" he said to the tree trunks, his square jaw set firmly. "Why don't you do what you're supposed to do? You don't just quit your job. You don't just walk away. You've got a goddamn family, for chrissake. You've got bills to pay. You don't just quit. You're the dad. Hell, even the stupid milkshake girl works more than you do!"

The trees said nothing in reply. They did, however, move in response to the wind that rolled across their tops just then. The naked alders less so. The breathy firs more so. Blue-eyed Paul felt satisfied that the forbidding woods of early winter offered this small acknowledgement. It helped to justify his resurgent feelings of rawness toward Lyle, and to forget even more thoroughly that he was there to hunt. The real hunt had nothing to do with bullets and beasts.

He furled his heavy brow and continued.

"Why the hell do you sit around with that look on your face?" Paul said to the sword ferns surrounding his knees. "Why don't you just get up off your ass and do something? Anything! But oh no. That's not gonna happen, now is it? No good sonofabitch. I mean sure, you did your part early on. Good for you. But then hell, you just up and fuckin' quit. And now you just sit around in the kitchen all depressed, lookin' like you don't have a goddamn clue about what to do. Do you realize how pathetic you are when your eyes are that empty? Yet you manage to keep that coffee cup nice and full. And who the hell do you suppose is paying for that coffee now? Well let me tell ya, old man. It sure as hell isn't you anymore! It's Mom. And you oughta be ashamed."

The dark green ferns dipped low to the sodden forest floor under the weight of the rain and the season, and not in deference to their tall, skinny visitor. But Paul saw it otherwise. Another wall of wind pushed through the treetops, causing every organic thing in his theatre of complaint to bow in a similar fashion. Looking up into the trees, he could no longer make out the clouds and that bothered him inside. The firs and the alders still had a collective silhouette, but they seemed to be fading into sameness as he watched. Returning his dilated eyes to the ground, Paul disliked how much less he could see. A tingling charge of distress emerged from the back of his armpits and crawled deliberately down the flesh that covered his triceps, escaping at his elbows.

Paul remembered his duty as a hunter. He shouldered his rifle and looked through his scope to see how much detail remained of the day. He scanned slowly to the right, trying not to let his breathing unsteady his view. The scope delivered more light to Paul's shooting eye than it could get on its own, so he could still make things out. If an animal presented itself, he would have a legal shot.

In that splendid moment of readiness, he saw something move in the distance. Something was out there with him. Slipping among the tree trunks. Dipping its head to avoid entanglements. Placing its hooves with precision. Breathing the air of the coming night, nostrils flaring, ears flicking, eyes on Paul.

He sensed he was being watched. And in the next instant, Paul realized that he could no longer see what he thought he saw. The light was too dim. His scope was useless. His rifle was much less of a weapon. He was every bit the non-hunter he had been before, only now the choice was not his: Paul had far less control over the woods than he had over his anger or imagination.

"Is it time to leave?" Paul whispered to the girl of his daydreams. "Do I go now? It feels like it's time. But Dad always says if there's a glimmer of light, there's a glimmer of hope. But man, I just don't know...."

His father's wisdom held Paul's boots firm on the soft and swollen ground. The issue was no longer how to hunt past twilight. The issue was how not to disappoint the impatient man who tried to teach his boys the tricks of hunting. Bail out too soon, Paul admonished himself, and Lyle gives him hell. Bail out too late, and he's walking out of the woods by Braille.

Paul's mind raced while his legs stood still. A stealthy herd of random ideas sprinted into and out of his consciousness. One was about the woods closing in on him. Another was about the time he stood up and announced to his fourth grade class that they should stop calling him Paulie. Yet another was about how many shades of dark exist in the unlit woods. Many other thoughts competed for his attention. But the one that held sway was the confusion Paul felt about Lyle. That one was bigger and stronger than any of the others, and it leapt higher and longer. At the very moment this idea stopped in the crosshairs of Paul's consciousness, it looked squarely into his eyes. He realized that of the two of them, he was the weaker.

Instantly, Paul could not breathe. His lungs were expelling a breath when they locked down, unable to continue or take in new air. His brain obliterated the herd of competing ideas so it could answer the question that suddenly mattered most:

"What was that!?" whispered Paul.

It took fractions of a second for his brain to catch up with events. It was a shot, his brain told him. Someone shot at something. You heard the bullet hit, said his brain. That sharp splat of impact. Then you heard the explosion of gunpowder, because you know how it is out here. The sound of impact beats the sound of the gun when fired in your direction, because the bullet goes faster than the speed of sound. That's what you just heard, said Paul's brain. Now get the hell out of here. Because somebody got a deer. Lyle did. And he needs your help. This hunt is done.

Paul's adrenaline-charged legs took over for his brain.

For a few brilliant minutes, he was as graceful and speedy at running through the treacherous woods as any animal. It was as if his body knew exactly which direction to go.

Cut right. Bolt left. Push through the bramble. Go over the rotten logs. Go, go, go, you sonofabitch! Don't you dare stop until you reach the fencerow. You can breathe later. Just fuckin' go, and get your soggy ass out of here. You're off the hook, boy. You're free.

The fence was the finish line. Paul crossed it with a relief that revealed how badly he wanted out of those woods. His heart pounded wildly from his thrashing exodus, yet it instantly began to calm as he pushed back through the barbed wire and into the pasture, where faint light still lingered. Paul looked down the fence to where Lyle and Bill went in, his eyes milking every last lumen. There they were. Right where they were supposed to be. Vague and colorless, perceptibly moving, the right sizes and shapes to be a man and a boy. But then, the larger shape began aggressively gesturing with an arm.

Paul froze.

He did not want to accept what his anxious eyes told him.

He resisted the idea that Lyle was signaling an instruction, which was this: go back into the dead woods of December.

Paul was crestfallen to realize he'd come up short in Lyle's distant eyes. He'd left the woods too soon. Cut the hunt short. Wasted the effort of going out on such a dreary day at all. Because at that one critical moment, when the light was all but gone and the deer felt safe, Paul wasn't where he needed to be.

"What about that shot I heard?" asked Paul of his milkshake girl. "I didn't imagine that!"

But he realized that only Lyle could have fired. He knew that because Lyle was already out of the woods and not tending to the meat, the shot had missed. And that buck? It was probably picking its way through the woods, heading straight for the spot where Paul was supposed to be, somehow sensing that its chances were better if it moved toward the lesser hunter. The one most likely to run.

Paul also knew exactly what would come from Lyle in the end. He pictured Lyle looking down at something, maybe his boots as he unlaced them, slowly shaking his head in dismay. He could hear the familiar words coming his way; spiteful, damning and, unbeknownst to Paul, self-deprecating:

"I teach you everything I know, and still you know nothing."

These anticipations launched Paul back through the barbed wire. He charged back into the deep and unwelcoming woods, retracing his steps as best he could. In a blurring surge of desperation, he went all the way back to the very site of his failure.

Now the ugly woods were uglier still. And this was Paul's punishment. To stand alone in the woods that he could no longer see. To feel the encroaching bleakness. To sense the awakening of inanimate things that were no longer required to be inanimate, because the daylight no longer stood sentry over them. To be tortured under his rain-soaked clothes by wave after wave of prickly discontent on his flesh, rolling across his humbled shoulders and reaching the length of his extremities like silent thunder, shocking him again and again as if to teach a very basic lesson: do what your old man tells you.

It was already too late to fix it. Paul knew it. But he did not know which frightened him more; being stuck out there as he was, or facing Lyle's disapproval as he eventually would. Neither option held promise.

Paul could no longer see a difference between the elements overhead. The trees and clouds had merged to eliminate all detail. His eyes ached at the lack of light. His free hand began to scan the hardening air like primitive radar, while his rifle hand stayed locked around the action. He knew there was no point in staying, and began lifting and planting his new boots in the direction he'd just come from, or so he hoped.

As he walked, the idea of not getting out occupied Paul's mind. It overpowered any sensations he got from his ears or his eyes or his radar hand or his dripping nose. The idea ballooned into melodrama: Paul tripping over something he could not see, falling hard on the sharp staub of a fallen tree, bleeding like a gut shot deer, dying instantly but not being found until hours later by searchers who brought bright flashlights and faint hopes, drawing friends and family to the memorial service that nobody wanted to attend because it just wasn't right....

Paul felt tears coming. Block that idea with a better one, he told himself. Keep walking out of the woods but change that tape. And then, his favorite new fantasy began to play:

§

It's a summer afternoon and t-shirt warm. Paul stands in the shade at the walk-up window at Haley's, the hamburger drive-in on the highway. He leans on the counter, right beside the Mason jar of straws and the chrome napkin dispenser. He waits for his root beer milkshake, which is being made by a short, cute blonde wearing a white waitress uniform.

She wears no slip. Every time she stands on her tiptoes and leans to see how the shake is doing, her uniform pulls tight to highlight her white bra and panties. Paul appreciates her, and does not mind that she is uncertain about when a shake is considered a shake. In fact, she is largely responsible for Paul ordering shakes at all, because he loves watching her. The windows of the drive-in are very clean. He sees her clearly, and feels a proximity that would not otherwise be possible, as she is two years older than Paul, and new in town, which means she doesn't officially know him.

The windows reflect the cars parked behind him, as well as the cars cruising by. Just as the cute blonde leans to take one last look, Paul sees the reflection of a little, red VW bug pulling in, the same one that starred in his previous favorite fantasy.

He sees shapes of girls inside—jostling heads of hair, narrow shoulders, angular arms, and big white smiles. And when the tweet-tweet sound of their exhaust pipes dies down, he hears their voices, their laughter. Scrutinizing their reflections, Paul sees that there are five of them. Five beautiful girls crammed into a red VW bug! The moment shoots adrenaline into his system.

"What do I do? What do I do?" he asks the milkshake girl, who now, in the cockeyed tradition of adolescent daydreams, is willing and able to address Paul.

"Are you kidding me?" she replies. "First I let you check me out through the window and now you want advice from me about them? As if I'm no longer good enough for you?"

Her words exasperate him.

"But you're the unattainable milkshake girl," says Paul. "And they're the five girls in the red VW I imagined before I even thought of you. Don't you see? I'll never get you, but now I've got a chance to get them."

The milkshake girl feigns a pout.

"There's your shake, heartbreaker."

Paul digs deep into his pockets for the seventy-five cents he owes.

"Nope," she says. "On the house, so long as you keep coming back to watch me through the window."

"Promise," says Paul.

"Now you better get over there before they go, because they didn't stop here for something to eat."

"They didn't?

"No, silly. They stopped for you."

Looking toward the red VW, Paul sees the passenger door open. The girl riding shotgun gestures for Paul to get in with the three backseat girls. He approaches and starts to say something, but the shotgun girl silences him with slender finger that goes perpendicular to her lips. Then she winks.

The back is very full of eyes and arms and breasts and naked knees. There is no place for him to be. Then he realizes that it's impossible for him to make a wrong move. That whatever he does, wherever he lands, whomever he touches, it will be okay. And if he gets an indelicate erection in the process, nobody will mind. Because these are the five girls. They know how it is for Paul. They know how he feels about things, about his life. And that knowledge makes it possible for them to welcome Paul into their circle, despite his youth and clumsy inexperience. They know they can trust him not to overstep. And the reward for knowing his place is to nestle in among them. And to be shown gentle kindnesses of improbable proportion. To ride with them in their little, red VW, at the expense of all other males on earth.

§

Whack!

A cold, wet, invisible branch slapped Paul hard on the right side of his face. It stung like hell. He hadn't seen it coming because his only vision was imaginary. And now, having reawakened to the sickly night woods, the fear returned.

Fear of being lost. Fear of being out there overnight. Fear of creatures he cannot see. Even fear of getting out, because that meant having to face his father. Although Paul realized he'd rather take the cussing than take his chances in the woods. No shame in taking the old man's crap, said the voice within. Everybody has to do it one way or another, and it sure beats the shit out of being known as the kid who went into the woods and never came out again. *Push on! Pretend you can see and push on. Fuck the unknown.*

Paul struggled against the night, the underbrush, a poor sense of direction, and the wicked elasticity of surreal time. Winded and weary, he remembered something Lyle taught him. The thing about stationary silence. So he stopped cold. He tried to hold his breath in order to hear what the woods had to say. But that was futile, because his lungs wanted air more than his ears wanted guidance. He stood there motionless until his chest stopped heaving. Then he listened. And he heard that the rain had completely stopped. He heard that the wind remained in the treetops. He heard the trees trying to rustle themselves dry, sending droplets to the sodden ground in a chorus of small thuds. He heard the pounding of his own heart, amplified by his own throat, broadcasting out his open mouth. He thought about how stupid and scared he would look if a light suddenly found him, and the image made him shut his mouth and begin walking again.

Suddenly, something attacked from the darkness, focusing all attention on Paul's right knee.

It tore through his jeans.

It gouged and gored and bored into his flesh.

It knocked him off balance, scraping and clawing at him, wanting his blood.

He fell awkwardly, and the burning pain jumped to his right elbow. Then to his shoulder. Then to the right side of his face, and his right ear. There was no time to think.

Then Paul heard his attacker, squeaking.

The sound of old bedsprings. Resonate metal-on-metal, screeching and squawking, but more random and maniacal.

Paul rebounded from his attacker's grasp and fell to the ground. His wounds roared at him. The warmth of his own blood shocked him…

But the next thing he felt brought sudden relief.

Grass.

Tall, dead grass.

The kind that grows along the fencerow separating the woods from the pasture.

"I'll be damned," he said out loud. "Walked right into the fuckin' bobwire."

Okay, he coached himself. I'm cut up, but this will work.

Paul knew to walk straight away from the fence through the pasture. There would be rise about a hundred yards out. And from that rise he'd be able to see the lights of their friends' house. That's where they parked the VW bus, and where he'd find Lyle and brother Bill.

They were waiting for him when he walked into the glorious light of the front porch.

"Look, dad!" said Bill. "He's bleeding!"

"What the hell, boy?" said Lyle. "Looks like somethin' got the best of *you*."

"Too dark to see," explained Paul. "Got tangled up in the fence."

"Dark is right," said Lyle. "You're kinda pushin' it there, aren't ya?"

"Man, your blood looks cool," gushed Bill.

"You signaled me to go back in!" exclaimed Paul to Lyle. "I saw you signal!"

"Huh, I wondered what you were up to out there," said Lyle, who calmly understood the miscommunication. "But listen, that wasn't a signal to turn around."

"But that's what you—"

"We were waving you in, Paulie." interrupted Bill. "Not waving you back."

"But—" said Paul.

"Your brother's right," said Lyle with a shrug. "I'm guessin' it was too dark for you to see the signal right."

All three of them went silent in the porch light for a moment, to absorb the facts. Then Paul continued.

"So, that was you doing the shooting?"

"Lousy little forked horn," answered Lyle. "Hardly big enough to bother with and runnin' away from me to boot."

"Dad missed," added Bill, who never passed up a chance to state the obvious.

"Huh," said Paul with a hint of satisfaction. "Okay."

"Man, I bet you feel stupid for getting Dad's signal completely wrong," said Bill. "I bet it was pretty scary. Did you get scared, Paulie? Did you get lost?"

"Did you ever think that people might get tired of your stupid-ass questions?" barked Paul with big brother authority. "And don't call me that."

"What? Paulie?" pressed Bill.

"Little jerk," sneered Paul.

Normally there would be hell to pay for taking such a tone. But Lyle let it slide. This puzzled Paul, as did the complete lack of criticism from Lyle about how the hunt ended.

"Let's load up and head for home, boys," said Lyle. "And be sure to empty that gun."

And with that, Paul's anger took the rest of the night off.

The Plight of Shiner Black

When raindrops hit the very peak of The Narrows Tavern, they have an equal chance of running off in any of four directions. Weathered green shingles tier down to aging cedar gutters on all sides. But not over the door, which has its own little roof. The doorknob shines from countless grasps.

The proprietor inside is well past her time to shine, but Ruthie has few regrets. Down the bar from her, a regular. Lester. A few others sit at unsteady tables. And around them all, the walls bear the haze of a million ricocheted clichés.

A serious young man walks in. Sits near Lester. Waits for the ice to melt. It does.

§

"Shiner Black shoulda lived alone. But the way things worked out, he had 'imself a wife and a son," said Lester. "Kinda weird how a guy like that ever got somebody to share a house with 'em, let alone a goddamn bed."

"Why's that?" I asked with calculated indifference.

"Partly 'cause he was an ornery little sawed-off sonofabitch. Which, when you stop to think about it, ain't much of a reason. Seein' as this canyon is loaded with ornery sonsabitches of all sizes who don't deserve anything better than their own company. So I suppose you'd have to lay a good share of the blame on the fact that ol' Shiner wasn't much to look at. Not that any of us are," said Lester.

"But this Shiner, he was something special?" I pried.

"Oh, Lord Jesus!" said Lester, a paunchy, red-nosed logger who was being aggressively aged by solitude and beer. "He wasn't just ugly. He was oogly."

"A face only a mother could—"

"Only if his mother was blinded by Calapooya joy juice," interrupted Lester with a grin. "I mean to tell ya, there was sumpthin' went seriously wrong when his daddy hung his britches on the bedpost and Mother Black gave 'em the nod. 'Cause from what I heard, that baby came right out of the hangar looking like the Lord never meant it to be. Why the ears alone were big enough to start the hospital nurses a yappin'. Big, floppy sonsabitches that started out high on the little bugger's head, and went way low, down toward his jaw. No lobes, either."

"They're called conjoined ears," I said with an impatience he could not see.

"They was normal looking people, his folks. Lived their whole lives here. But Lord help 'em, they made one homely human being when they made Shiner Black. And I'll just betcha them old folks spent many a dark hour a wonderin' how the hell it was that they should produce such a misbegotten soul."

"Misbegotten, huh?" I said, realizing how uncomfortable it makes me when people like Lester use words that aren't theirs.

As summer darkness approached, most customers of The Narrows had trickled out through the open doors. A few regulars stayed on, drinking cold beer and swatting at mosquitoes. Lester stayed on because the tired tavern was his home. I stayed because of Lester.

"Listen, kid," said Lester. "I pro'bly shouldn't be tellin' you this, 'cause it ain't nice to talk about the de-ceased and all. On the other hand—"

"You bought the beer, big man."

"Okay. Well. Here's the thing about Mr. Valentine Shiner Black."

"Yeah?"

"Well," said Lester as he leaned toward me to whisper, "they say he was a numb face."

"A numb face," I repeated flatly.

"Yep, they say he couldn't feel a thing from the neck up. So that little varmint couldn't feel a goddamn thing. Which ya gotta admit is purdy unusual."

"Helluva thing," I said innocently.

"Yep, and there ain't nobody knows the cause, 'cept maybe Shiner himself, and word is he never talked about it."

"That right."

"Yep, he didn't do much talkin' at all, 'cept when he was fixin' to fight. And Christ, you shoulda see 'um. Pick a fight with anyone, he would. Didn't matter how much bigger they were. Didn't matter if he was outnumbered. Because 'ol Shiner had himself a secret weapon."

"A face that could feel no pain," I said.

"Well of course, that's where it started. But think it through. Whadaya suppose would be the biggest benefit of feeling no pain? What'd Shiner Black have that almost nobody else in the whole misbegotten motherfuckin' world had?"

"How about a complete lack of fear?" I said.

With that, Lester bolted straight up from his bar stool, bringing his untethered belly from its customary position beneath the counter to a much more pronounced position above the counter, his massive, thickly callused hands planted firmly on the layers of shellac that shielded the wooden counter from years of beers, his huge neck crooked in the direction of the chain-smoking barmaid down the way.

"Ruthie, old girl! Hey, Ruthie! Bring my friend here a brand new Blitz. For he's a bright and sober young man who deserves nothing but the wettest of whistles. On my tab, if you please. And while you're at it, another for your best customer."

I pretended to be embarrassed by Lester's theatrics, and dipped my head toward the bar. Then I recovered by suggesting it was my turn to buy.

"I insist," I said with a muffled voice. "Besides, seems like this place gets the better part of your paycheck as it is."

"I'll drink to that," said Lester.

We fell momentarily silent in the tavern, but for no particular reason other than to await the arrival of Ruthie with two fresh beers. She was an artificial redhead who looked to be sixty or so, with a face that reserves its ability to smile for those times that really warrant it, for those people who really inspire it. This was not one of those times. Lester was not one of those people. And as far as I could tell in the fading evening light, neither was I. She put down the beers without making eye contact or saying a word. Then she shuffled to the opposite end of the counter, where she filed her nails without conviction, smoking all the while.

"That Ruthie," said Lester in low voice. "She's been a pourin' beer here since the mountains got made. And she used to be a real looker, too. Kind of a happy thing. Always a whistlin' or a singin' something to herself. But that's been a while."

"They say time heals all wounds, but I say time takes its toll," I said.

"Time and people," countered Lester.

"Yeah? How so?"

"Well, in the case a Ruthie here, she's seen a lot from the backside of this bar. Lot of rough characters. Lot of trouble. Lot of people just flat out fallin' apart right before 'er eyes. And, I might add, she's had her share of experience with ol' Numb Face."

"He used to come here? He was a regular?"

"Not a regular like I'm a regular. But there was a time when he use ta show up here often enough. Just like he use ta show up at The Alders, and Lorna's and the Widowmaker Inn. Trouble was, sumpthin' always happened that made it so Shiner weren't welcome any one place for any length of time."

"A fight?"

"That'd be typical. Like the time he was sittin' not two stools down from where you are right now, drinking like it was Friday night on a Tuesday. I was sittin' right here, so I seen everything."

"Uh-huh."

"This fella named Ivan Thrower comes in the place, all dressed to the nines after goin' to see the Chevy dealer down the way about a salesman job, which it turns out he got. So Thrower, he saunters in here all gussied up and smellin' of Old Spice, actin' kinda cocky. White shirt with a turquoise bolo tie. Creased slacks. Hair all slicked back and shiny with pomade. I tell ya, that boy was a spectacle."

"Especially in a place like this," I said.

"Oh-ho yes. So ol' Shiner, he manages to ignore Ivan Thrower for a good long while. But Thrower's no wallflower, and it ain't long before he's the loudest sonofabitch in the place, talkin' it up with whoever'd play along, but mostly with Ruthie here. And Shiner, he's gettin' kinda twitchy, listenin' to Mr. High-and-Mighty go on and on about how he's gonna be sellin' Impalas and Corvairs, and how he's fine-ly getting' out of his lousy job down at the plywood mill. How he's gonna tell his foreman to take a flyin' fuck and all. You know?"

"Oh yeah, I know."

"Yeah, there was no shortage of things for Shiner to get upset about. But whadaya 'spose got to Numb Face that night?"

I let my expression tell Lester that I had no clue.

"Shoes," said Lester. "Shiner Black decided he had to do sumpthin' about Ivan Thrower's shoes."

"Shoes…"

"Yeah, some kinda patent leather dancin' shoes. Shiny as a new Chevy. So ol' Shiner, he's leanin' forward on his elbows on the bar. And he kinda hooks his goofy little head so he can see the floor under his right arm. The rest of him was still square to the bar. And he's just a starin' at them fancy black shoes. And then he starts mumblin' sumpthin' I couldn't quite make out."

"Fancy Pants heard him?"

"I believe so. 'Cause Thrower, he kinda squares up to Shiner, and he says sumpthin' like 'What was that, little fella?' And Shiner, he lifts his head up out of his armpit, and he says so everybody can hear that Ivan Thrower looks like a Portland pimp."

"Fightin' words," I said.

"You can bet the Bel Air on that. And it sure as hell lit a fire under Ivan. 'Cause the next thing ya know, he took Shiner right off his stool and threw him hard against that pool table right there," said Lester with a gesture over his shoulder.

"Everybody else just watched?"

"Oh hell yeah. Ain't nothin' more entertainin' than a good tavern fight."

"Especially when Shiner Black's involved, I suppose."

"Specially."

"So how'd it come out? Who won the fight?"

"Oh, Ivan Thrower did," said Lester. "But the way he won kinda got him in hot water with folks around here. Now understand, weren't nobody surprised that ol' Shiner got his ass kicked again. That's normal. But it ain't normal for someone to pull a switchblade and start a carvin' on poor ol' Shiner's face. Which is what happened.

"And when word got out, people didn't like the idea. So ol' Thrower never managed to sell a single goddamn Chevy. And Shiner, he just went on home and got his wife to throw a few stitches in his face."

"Man, I dunno," I said to keep him talking. "Take a special kind of woman to put up with shit like that. And for what? Because I mean, there's not much chance a guy's gonna get less ugly when they turn out the lights."

"Oogly."

"Exactly," I said, sensing Lester's reluctance to answer the question.

Lester lifted his elbows off the counter and straightened his back. He reached toward the dingy ceiling, stretching, dropping his head to tighten the muscles at the base of his large skull, unfolding the skin of his fleshy neck, opening his right eye to squint at his soon-to-be-empty beer glass.

"C'mon, Ruthie!" he said loudly. "You're fallin' behind."

The haggard barmaid did not acknowledge Lester.

"She ignoring us?" I asked.

"She's pissed," whispered Lester.

"At us?"

"Me, mostly. Maybe a little at you."

"What'd *we* do?"

"Shit fire, it don't take much to catch heck around here. But this time, I think ol' Ruthie here has picked up a little too much of our conversation," said Lester as he settled back down onto the counter.

He grabbed his beer glass and smacked the heavy base of it smartly on the wooden counter. Ruthie relented, pouring two more glasses of Blitz and then sliding them in front of us. As she glided back to her side of the room, Lester continued.

"I figure she knows we're talking about Shiner Black. No big deal. But she also musta heard you just askin' about Shiner's wife."

"So?"

"So Ruthie, she don't like Mrs. Black. Got no use for the woman ay-tall."

"Uh-oh," I said, sensing a turn in the story.

"Yeah, that's right."

"She had a thing for Shiner? Well I'll be damned."

"More than a thing! She dumped her husband for 'em. Kicked him right out the front door with nothin' more than a suitcase and an overcoat. Boom."

"And Shiner left his wife?"

"By all accounts, he had no desire to leave 'er. They say he was crazy 'bout that Nancy. Do anything for 'er. Whatever she said. Whatever she wanted."

"So our friendly neighborhood barmaid got the short end of the stick."

"Short 'n' sharp, my friend. Short 'n' sharp. But that was only after three years a Shiner climbin' all over her in the storeroom back there, where she kept 'erself a cot. And used to be they'd wait 'til the place cleared out, then they'd go back there 'n' tear it up a little. An' remember, this was back when Ruthie was a finer lookin' woman."

"Okay, but help me out with something, Lester."

"Yessir."

"How'd you know what was going on in the back room? Because you're a little too large to be a fly on the wall."

"Well, I may be a load. But I'm a quiet one. An' the fact is, I flat out caught 'em at it one time."

"Hmmm."

"Yeah, I'd gone out the door with a couple other fellas who were headin' home. But I was just pissin' in the parkin' lot. And when I come back in to finish up my Blitz, Ruthie and Shiner was nowhere in sight. Well the next thing I know, I hear some mighty funny sounds comin' from the back. So I snuck around behind the bar and poked my head through the doorway. An' by then I kinda had me an idea of what was goin' on."

"And they didn't hear you coming?"

"Hell no," said Lester with sneer. "That little floppy-eared bastard had his pants down to his boots, justa goin' to town on Ruthie. And she was gigglin' like a goddamn schoolgirl, she was. And that goddamn cot was just a screeching an' a squeakin' an' a slidin' all over the storeroom. Shit was a fallin' off the shelves. And them two didn't have a clue about me."

"You paint a vivid picture, Lester."

"Well, it ain't the kinda thing a fella can easily ferget. And truth be told, I always kinda regretted seein' Shiner Black's bare ass."

"I'll drink to that," I said.

"Me, too."

"So, did Nancy Black ever find out about what was going on in the backroom of the infamous Narrows Tavern?"

"Funny you should ask. 'Cause ol' Nancy *did* get wind of it," said Lester, who then lowered and muffled his voice again so as not to be heard by Ruthie. "An' I'm the one who told 'er."

"You!?"

"I know. I know. Sounds kinda terrible don't it? But I didn't have no particular problem or score to settle with Shiner. Or Ruthie."

"What the hell happened?"

"See, the thing is, it was Nancy that set the wheels a turnin'. And I just kinda got in the way. Or maybe I should say I had me one helluva time tryin' to get outta the way."

"I'm lost, Lester."

"She was a man-eater, man."

"Nancy Black?"

"Damn right. A regular black widow. And I was one a her victims."

"You?"

"Yeah, me. And the whole thing got started one night up at The Alders, that beer joint just upstream a town. I was in there on a Friday night, drinkin' Blitz and shootin' some pool with some boys I know. And in comes Shiner and Nancy, like they was on a date or sumpthin'.

"But Nancy, she's a big ass flirt. And it didn't take but twenty minutes before she'd managed to make Shiner jealous 'cause a sumpthin' some poor fella said in response to a look Nancy put out in his general di-rection. And Shiner bein' Shiner, he lit into the other fella like he had nothin' to lose. But nobody won that fight, 'cause the owner, he pulls out this Louisville Slugger from behind the counter and runs the both a them right out the door, right into their rigs, and right down the road. 'Cept Nancy, she don't go with Shiner."

"The hell."

"Nope, she stayed on without 'em. And the next thing I know, she's sidlin' up beside me, wantin' to shoot my shots on the pool table. Wantin' to sip my beer. Bumpin' into me with her hips in that dress that showed off what a fine little waist she still had."

"So you fell victim to the wily ways of a woman looking for trouble."

"Now listen. I'm a man of principle for the most part. I know right from wrong. But I been a bachelor a long goddamn time. And I ain't never been much to look at. So when something that nice comes my way…."

"You played along."

"You're goddamn right I did. I mean Christ! I may be a little misbegotten myself. But I ain't stupid."

"So you and Nancy, you carried on a little."

"For a couple a months, I reckon. But I ain't the only one. 'Cause that damn Nancy, she had a knack for sniffin' out just about any man with a long leash. And I think she liked the extra attention. So I didn't last all that long with her."

"She got bored?"

"And I got scared."

"So how'd you come to tell her about Shiner and Ruthie?"

"Hmm, well, let's just say she wiggled it outta me."

"Okay, okay. Nancy's a piece of work. You're a horny bachelor. Shiner's a fearless runt. And Ruthie's a heartsick barmaid. But I'm still kinda lost in the dark here, and I keep bumping into questions...."

"Like what?," said Lester.

"Well first off, if Shiner was so dedicated to Nancy, why was he sneaking around with Ruthie?"

"Hell's bells, boy. All I can figure is that even though he musta loved her beyond all hope or reason, he pro'bly needed to get even, ya know? Make 'er pay."

"All right. Fine. But how do you suppose it is that a man as ugly and disagreeable as Shiner Black managed to have two decent looking women in his life? I mean, geez, most guys are lucky to find one."

Lester took a long, gulping drink from his beer glass until it was drained. Then he set the empty on its side on the counter and gave it a brisk spin.

"Way I see it, there ain't much more to this whole business than a game a spin the bottle. The love compass ends up pointin' at you, then you're gonna get all tangled up with someone. If it don't, then you're gonna go on alone for the most part. Like Ruthie here. Like me.

"Now in the case a Shiner Black, looks like the compass mighta got stuck for a while. So he gets the attention of Nancy and Ruthie, even though he ain't got much goin' for him."

"Excuse me, Lester," I said. "I don't mean to offend, but that's a weak explanation."

"Hey, maybe I'm right. Maybe I'm wrong. But that's how I see it. And I figure that's about all the explanation a person oughta expect from a fella whose main goal in life is keepin' taverns in business."

"Point taken."

"Thank you kindly."

Lester raised his empty as high as his massive arm could lift it, holding it there until Ruthie got the message. We took another break from our conversation while the woman who used to have a cot in the backroom brought another round. She continued to ignore Lester, but this time she looked me squarely in the eyes. Then, as before, she floated off to the opposite end of the counter. She retrieved a crossword from beneath the black phone on the bar and left the room.

"But still," I continued. "What did these women see in Shiner Black that made it so they could look past his flaws?"

"Well now here's a thought," said Lester, who remained unsuspicious of me. "Maybe Nancy knew she's a terrible, manipulatin', heart-breakin' sort of woman. Maybe she knew herself inside and out. So maybe she realized from the very start that the only way she could get a man to actually stay with her was to pick on one that ain't likely to have many options. So's no matter what she did to 'em, or who she carried on with, the stupid sonofabitch would always be there to take 'er back.

"And as for ol' Ruthie here, well, maybe she's the opposite kinda woman. Maybe the only goddamn thing she's guilty of is having a kind heart. So's while Nancy saw Shiner as someone to run, Ruthie saw 'im as someone to save. Ugly as he was."

"Oogly," I said.

"Oogly as he was," said Lester with a grin.

"So what about Nancy and Ruthie? They ever get into it?"

"And then some. But not in a way you'd expect. 'Cause as it happened, the beauty parlor that puts the red in Ruthie's hair is the same place that put the blonde in Nancy's hair. So one Saturday mornin' they both show up at the same time for a tune up. And from what I heard, they's both a sittin' there in that small room, justa starin' at each other without sayin' a word, with their hair all tangled up in dye and whatnot.

"Then Jane the beautician, she accidentally drops sumpthin' on the floor, and it makes a big ol' noise. And that's all she took for Nancy to come up flyin' outta her chair and starta slappin' Ruthie for all she's worth.

"But Nancy was no match for a woman who makes her livin' behind a bar. So ol' Ruthie came right back at 'er with the force of righteous vengeance, just like in the Bible. And she whupped Nancy Black right then and there. Flattened 'er out but good. Hair dye and beauty equipment was a flyin' in all directions. And when the fight was over, roughhouse Ruthie here was the only one standin'."

"Two women fighting over the oddest little man in the canyon," I observed.

"And ol' Nancy, she's the one went home with a shiner."

"Ha!" I said, fully appreciating the delicious irony of it all and grinning my sly grin.

"Yessir," affirmed Lester, grinning the same grin.

Ruthie, who'd said nothing all evening, suddenly appeared in front of us with a white bar towel over her shoulder. She tapped her wristwatch and said, "Last round." She lifted her manufactured eyebrows and dropped her chin slightly to inquire whether or not we wanted one for the road. We responded with nods that said yes.

"You said he had a son. What became of *him*?" I asked as Ruthie fetched the beer.

"It ain't too surprisin', all things considered," said Lester. "The boy run off a long time ago. Barely old enough to shave. Flat out disappeared."

"Yeah?"

"Yeah. And there was talk at first that maybe he got himself kidnapped or killed or sumpthin' like that. But that was just talk. 'Cause they never could come up with a solid explanation of what became of the kid. And then, after a few years a him bein' gone, people just kinda quit talkin' about 'im. Like the young fella never existed in the first place."

"Helluva thing."

"Mysterious as all get out," affirmed Lester. "Which was pretty much opposite of the situation surrounding ol' Shiner's death. No mystery there."

"I suppose the State Police were all over that one, weren't they," I speculated.

"And I don't rightly blame 'em. Specially the corporal in charge. 'Cause if it hadn't been for Shiner Black, that poor sonofabitch woulda spent the better part of his career playin' game warden up here, tryin' to catch up to poachers who're gen'rally a lot smarter than him."

"Yeah?"

"Yeah, but that corporal caught himself a bigass break when Nancy took care a Shiner. One mighty swing a that cast iron fryin' pan, and Corporal Whatshisname became Sergeant Whatshisname," said Lester.

"Death can be a blessing, I hear."

Lester laughed a little at that. "Yeah. Specially when you ain't the one doin' the dyin'."

"Here, here."

"Of course, they wrote it up as self-defense," said Lester with a tone of doubt.

"But you don't buy it."

"Not for goddamn second. 'Cause Nancy Black was as crafty as they come. Slippery smart and all fer 'erself."

"So tell me, Lester. What's your theory of the crime? How'd this caper go down?"

"Well it sure as hell don't take a drunken genius like yours truly to figure it out. 'Cause if ya know anything about the Blacks at all, it's plain to see that Shiner was ripe for the pickin', and Nancy was geared up for the harvest. She knew ev'rybody knew about Shiner's taste for fightin'. She knew ev'rybody thought he was a little bit crazy.

"So she figures, 'what the hell, I'll just bring my cookin' skills to bear on poor Shiner's skull. Whack 'em good, and then tell ev'ryone he was in a terrible rage and tryin' to do me harm.'

"That's when I figure Nancy did the big sell job on the corporal. 'Cause as good as Shiner was at findin' trouble, Nancy was better at talking her way outta trouble."

"Sounds like it worked, I guess."

"Never even charged 'er."

"And the night she killed her own husband, she got to sleep in her own bed?"

"Like a baby, I reckon."

"Unbelievable," I said.

We both took long, slow swallows of our last beer of the night. Our beer glasses came down solidly on the wooden counter, almost in unison. We both exhaled audibly, leaning on our elbows, momentarily staring at the beer taps on the wall behind the counter. Ruthie drifted into our view with a bar towel, wiping the taps and putting them to bed for the night.

"Ohhh, Nancy," said a suddenly wistful Lester.

"Yeah," I followed. "What became of Nancy Black? You said she split the canyon once she was cleared?"

"Frisco."

"San Francisco?" I said. "You know, people there really hate it when you call it Frisco."

"Uh-huh. Well I reckon someone down there didn't much care for the way Nancy said it either."

"Huh."

"Yeah, she moved on down there after Shiner. After the trouble. Got a room in some place called Richmond."

"Oh. The East Bay. Not San Francisco," I corrected.

"Whatever you say. But the point ain't so much where she lived as where she died."

"Her, too?"

"Damn straight. Right there in a crosswalk, just in front that department store called Macy's. Some guy apparently laid 'er out flat on the pavement with a Plymouth or sumpthin'. Boom!" said Lester as he clanked his glass into mine, recreating the moment. "Hit an' run, 'cordin' to the paper."

"That's a lonely way to go, dying in the city."

Lester snickered a small snicker, dropping his head a little toward the counter. "*Hell*uva way to go. But I reckon it was the right way for Nancy. Her pro'bly bein' all sprawled out there on her back, her dress jacked up over 'er head where it ain't spose to be, makin' a spectacle of herself, drawin' attention."

"You're saying the penalty fit the crime?"

"Naw, young fella. I ain't in no position to be sayin' anything like that. But I am sayin' that it's mighty damn strange how things come around sometimes."

"Full circle, you're saying."

"There ya go. Full circle," said Lester.

"You know what I think?" I said, picking up on Lester's philosophical tone. "I think everybody might've had Shiner Black wrong."

"Oh, I dunno 'bout that, boy," countered Lester. "Whatcha saw was whatcha got."

"Maybe it was only what you *thought* you got, Lester. Maybe it turns out that the man who couldn't feel a thing could actually feel everything. Maybe he felt too much, you know? Maybe that's why he got the way he got. Maybe he just decided to be numb."

"Well, maybe," said Lester, who was instantly tired of the whole topic. "But who the hell gives a shit?"

Ruthie reappeared before us, now wearing a blue summer sweater over her work clothes. She was ready to go home, and invited us to do the same.

Lester stood up from his barstool with a degree of difficulty. Back pain showed on his face. But he gathered himself up and headed for the door. I followed with much less ceremony. Lester was already outside as I stepped across the threshold, the doorknob in my hand. I was stopped by Ruthie's voice.

"I know who you are. I know everything worth knowing about you, 'cause your old man told me," said Ruthie. "He told me you were as crazy as he was homely, and twice as wicked as your mother. He told me you'd show up one dark day, and there'd be hell to pay."

I did not respond, choosing instead to fix on her eyes.

"Leave Lester be. You've got no real score to settle with him, 'cause he's just another one of your mother's victims. Just like you. So here's your chance to leave this canyon and stay invisible. That is, unless you've got plans for me, too."

I stood for another moment in the threshold without saying a word. Then I stepped on through, still looking. I pulled the door slowly toward me. I used the edge of the door to sever the eye contact between us. I spun on the doorstep. Then I counted each of the twenty-three paces it took to reach the front of my Plymouth—the one I took down to San Francisco.

"Oh, I've got plans," I said in delayed response to Ruthie. "And everybody gets to play."

§

Ruthie picks up the black phone at the end of her sorry bar. She peers through a slit in the curtains on the door, keeping an eye on the son of Shiner Black. She dials.

"Sergeant? It's your old friend at The Narrows."

She waits for his unoriginal greeting.

"Oh, it's goin' just fine. But listen sergeant, you really oughta come down here right now."

She absorbs his predictable question with a nod.

"Well, let's just put 'er this way: If you do, we're pro'bly gonna be callin' you lieutenant before deer season. Or at least before the rains come."

The River Likes to Win

The moss was drier than Jack expected for December. Thick and ancient, it covered the rock that held the camp. He thought of it as his camp. His rock. Because it was his place to go when the need arose. His place to take only those he chose.

It had a proper geographic place name. But to use that name would have been to surrender his right to sanctuary there, because the long-forgotten place could be discovered by anyone capable of using a good map. This would have been unacceptable to Jack, who was never absolutely sure who else might know of the camp. He rarely said the name aloud.

All he knew was that in all the times he went there, he never once encountered anyone else who hadn't been with him. Nor had he ever seen signs that anybody else had been there since he last visited.

The game trail that crept up through the woods on the backside of the massive rock knob was obscure. The trailhead changed in appearance from season to season—even Jack sometimes made a wrong turn getting started, and that pleased him, because he knew confusion was an excellent sentry.

December made the trail slightly easier to find this time, because the tall grass and leggy ferns of summer had withered, and the embrace of briars had weakened. Once past the point of entry, the familiar old trail greeted Jack warmly. Bare dirt and rocks all in a row, slicing across the steep, tree-covered slope. Jack was fit, but the climb still had him breathing through his mouth.

At a point about three-quarters the way to the top, the trail intersected with another. To go straight was to battle the tight, gnarly underbrush decorating the ridge top running out to the west. Jack always turned right, north toward the moss.

The perpendicular trail followed a seam in the gigantic rock. An ascending, angular shelf. A track no wider than boots. On each visit, it brought Jack out of the dense woods and into the open, reintroducing him to the sky, which often prompted Jack to say hello and thanks, whatever the weather.

Cresting the top of the rock, Jack always made a small ceremony out of entering what he'd long called the Camp of the Gods. A flat, elegant circle of rich emerald moss, maybe fifteen feet at its widest point, surrounded by the brittle beauty of waist-high manzanitas, the dark red sculpture of their defiant limbs doing double duty as perimeter fence and decoration. And at the center, a small fire pit that Jack had made of rocks on his very first visit, when he was all of ten. Looking out from the center, Jack's view over the top of the manzanitas varied little. The tops of trees growing on the flanks of the rock. Douglas fir, mostly. And above the trees, mountaintops in three directions. And above the mountains, on this occasion, a homogenous gray sky. Standing there, feeling cradled by his stadium of nature, Jack always felt a little better. But this was not where the true work was done, because he knew that to see the actual nature of things, he must always approach the leading edge of the rock. And he knew she'd be waiting for him this time. There on the precipice.

Pushing through the manzanitas just opposite the point where he entered the Camp of the Gods, the rest of the world came into view. It was an immense topographical exhibition. A map of Jack's life in relief. Mountains and ridges in full view. Some covered with trees. Others scraped clean by landslides or clear-cut by loggers. Still others burnt by a decades-old fire, but in recovery. There were distant waterfalls that made no sound. There were ravines and draws and saddles and basins. And every bit of it was lit in a flat, shadowless monotone by the featureless cloud cover; typical for a late afternoon in December, in the mossy part of Oregon.

Looking down over the edge of the rock, Jack saw that the river was still there, still flowing by, five hundred feet below. An unrelenting waterbeast, bullying its way down the canyon. Dark green and angry. Grumbling about having been dammed upstream. Openly celebrational about having been set free to once again scour the land as it descends toward the distant Pacific. The thrashing power of frigid water in constant motion. True to itself every inch of the way. Never wavering from its mission, which amounted to nothing more than disagreeing with whatever or whoever challenged its authority. Its territorial imperative. Its force.

The sight of it always frightened Jack a little and humbled him a lot. Even as a young boy, he knew that any sense of superiority he might feel over the river came strictly as a consequence of his height above it, his safe distance from it. It was false confidence, because he knew that when he was eye-to-eye with the river, right at the surface, he was barely in charge of his own well-being. And beneath the surface, he knew the cold and the current would toy with him and then take him, just as it had unmercifully taken so many before.

On the entire run of the river, from its snowmelt sources high in the Cascade Mountains to its downstream merger with its sister rivers, there was no angrier or more violent place than the one immediately below Jack's camp. It's where, millions of years before, a flow of ambitious but misguided lava tried to block the river. It failed, but not before narrowing this ill-mannered whitewater monster to the insulting width of just four feet at the surface.

It was obvious to Jack that the river had enjoyed a big laugh at the expense of this rocky challenger, because rather than trying to flow over the natural dam, it went under. Coming downstream in a straight shot against the rocks, it coiled itself in a tight left-hand turn, then again in a sharp right-hand turn as it confronted the narrows. And then it dived beneath its own frothy, churning surface. It went forty feet down. It grew to a width of twenty-five feet at the bottom, which was more than adequate for the indifferent river to muscle through.

And then, as if to taunt the unsuccessful effort of the rocks, the river roiled through on the other side in a maniacal kaleidoscope of insane upswells and consumptive whirlpools, dancing and slapping itself with an arrogance that should never be underestimated or dismissed, because the river likes to win.

Jack stood at the edge with his legs apart, his arms crossed, the collar of his coat turned up against the occasional chill of the wind. The sound of the rapids and river churn seemed distant and delayed, a mighty creature held at arm's length by a nineteen-year-old who wondered whether he'd ever be the master of anything, and whether he'd know when he was a man and no longer a boy. He disliked the uncertainty of being midstream.

His arms lacked his father's burly hair. His body was trim and lean, and not all that muscular. He sprouted up to the satisfying height of five foot ten when he was just twelve, but then grew no more. His dark head of hair was short and groomed. His eyebrows were thick for someone so young, which collaborated with his black plastic eyeglasses to dominate the landscape of his face. His eyes were brown and honest. His smile charmed his mother when Jack was an infant, and later charmed the girls. One in particular.

He took his usual walk along the spine of the rock, to the east and somewhat downhill from the camp. He did this to make sure nothing had changed since he'd gone away for his first term at college. That everything was as it should be, as it had always been. Things looked right, so Jack returned to the high end, where the view had fewer obstructions. He found his spot, and he sat down on the moss with his lower back snug against a small, flat spot of the behemoth rock; his conversation chair. She was already there, ready to start.

"Who the hell ARE you?" she said like a careerist prosecutor making a statement disguised as a question.

"Who the hell am I?" he repeated defensively. "Who the hell am I? Who the hell are you?"

"I am who I've always been. Me. Right down the line."

"Same goes for me," said Jack.

"Bullshit."

"Hey!"

"I don't care," she said. "What you just said is bullshit, Jack. You aren't the same since you went away. You've changed. And I don't like it. Not at all."

"That's nuts," said Jack weakly.

"Hell it is, Jack."

"Stop cussing at me."

"How about you stop telling me what to do, Mr. My-Future's-More-Important-Than-Anything-Or-Anyone. Because I'll cuss if I want to, and there's not a goddamned thing you can do about it. Jesus, Jack, don't be such a big baby."

Wounded, Jack turned his blank eyes away, avoiding her. He let out a heavy, breathy sigh, collected himself, and then returned with a conciliatory tone.

"What are we fighting about?" he asked.

"Oh, we're not fighting yet. This is nothing."

"No. I mean, we never used to be like this. We always used to get along so well. You and me, we used to be easy. We used to be good."

"For cryin' out loud, Jackson. Will you pay attention?! This is us right now. This is how we *are*. This is what we've *got*. And you're not helping things by sittin' there whining."

"Stop it," said Jack quietly.

"Stop what? Telling the truth? Being honest?"

"Sopbeansohmeen," mumbled Jack.

"What'd you say?"

"I said, stop being so mean," he said.

"Mean! Me?"

"Yes, you."

"Oh, you're a fine one to talk. You treated me like shit for a month after I went to that party. You wouldn't speak to me. And when you did talk, you were one cold-hearted bastard. And you were totally willing to let me feel guilty about it when there was no real reason to. THAT'S mean, Jack. You've been mean to me."

"Hey, if you felt guilty about something, well—"

"You can't do that, Jack. You can't control me. I won't let you, 'cause it was just a goddamn kiss, okay? And the world didn't come to an end."

"You shouldn't have gone to the party, though. You shoulda stayed home."

"And save myself for what? For you?"

"Well?"

"Well what?" she barked.

"Well, isn't that how it's supposed to work? Isn't that our deal? We wait for each other? We avoid those kinds of situations?"

"KEE-riced! I can't believe what I'm hearing," she said, making no attempt to hide her disgust. "You're the one who went off to college. You're the one who never writes. You're the one who never calls. And even when you do call, you don't even sound like yourself, Jack. You don't even know what to say to me. So don't you dare talk to me about our deal, 'cause you broke it, jocko. You smacked it hard and broke it good. Kiss or no kiss."

"But you're the one who went to the party," he said in an attempt to suggest that wisdom and logic was on his side.

"Okay! I went to the goddamned party. So I drank too much and got a little too chummy with what's his name. So what? I can't just sit around brushing my hair, waitin' for you to call. I'd go insane."

"Urallredyinsane," mumbled Jack.

"There goes Mumblejack again. Can't quite say what he means. Doesn't have the balls to stand his ground. Well guess what, bumbledick. I don't really care what you're trying to say, because I don't believe I have the time."

And with that parting shot, she was gone from the mossy outlook. Jack shouted his response out over the river canyon.

"You're already insane, crazy bitch!"

Jack imagined his words echoing back to him, prompting him to nod in full agreement, gratified that at least the canyon understood.

The altercation left him weary. Numb. He stared across the canyon, studying the impassive tall firs in the distance. He wondered what they could hear from their position. What they could see. What they might say about his situation. What advice they might offer.

Realizing the irrelevance of such questions, Jack's eyes wandered to the biggest of three waterfalls he could see: Flowing big from early December rain, pure white and falling straight, bound for the river and points beyond, doing what it's supposed to do, having no questions, answering only to gravity; a clean, straightforward assignment Jack envied.

His eyes drifted down from the distant view to the one just below his boots. A structural shelf just a few feet down the face of the rock. Still mossy. Still with a view. But cozy and sheltered. Jack remembered how he and two childhood buddies spent an afternoon there once, perched on that shelf, telling stories about adventures yet to happen. He remembered how they built a small fire right there on the face. How they got a good bed of coals underneath a teepee of drying wood. How they each had an apple in their pocket. How they halved the apples and tried to roast them on sticks: an attempt at a fine hot meal in the wilds.

Jack remembered how they never got to eat their meal, because as they talked and laughed and roasted their apples, a sly blacktail doe slipped in behind them, following their path through the Camp of the Gods, through the grabby manzanita bushes, right out to the edge, right over them, looking down at them to see what was going on, just ten feet from them. Jack couldn't remember who saw the doe first. But it didn't matter. Because all three boys jumped straight up in the air —a festival of cats and firecrackers—in reaction to a pair of wild eyes having come in that close. Two of the boys landed solidly on the shelf with hearts pounding. But Jack lost his footing and went over the mossy face, coming down hard against the base of a young fir tree. It happened fast, and Jack didn't get hurt. But by the time he crawled back up to their fire, the doe was a mile gone. The boys were left with a real story to tell....

Jack continued sitting there.

He noticed it was getting colder, and the clouds were getting lower and darker. He began wishing it was summer, and that the nighthawks would come out for their evening meal, as he had seen them do many times before. Sleek, beautiful birds riding the last thermals of the day, high over the river canyon and nearly motionless, save for the slight tipping of one wing and then the other to correct for changes in the air. It wasn't so much the visual drama of the dive that captured Jack, though it was always fast and emphatic. It was the sound. Because once a nighthawk sets its sights on an insect in flight, it folds its narrow slicing wings tight against its body, using only the feathers it needs to aim itself toward its prey. Gravity and aerodynamics create downward speed. The movement of air around the gray-winged, white-bellied bird is an unmistakable sound. A compressed, low-pitched, purring kind of *whoosh*. It was enchanting for Jack but ominous for the insects—the sound meant life and death.

Jack thought about death. How people die a lot in the river canyon where he grew up. Mostly loggers in the woods, or motorists on the highway that runs along the river. The cemetery was full of sad, sudden stories. There was Ernie Fish, who Jack's dad had known as a kid. Ernie was from a big family of wild-ass boys. He wasn't the wildest. But what got him in trouble was that he also wasn't the smartest, which explains how it was that he figured to be safe taking an old wooden rowboat through the narrows beneath Jack's camp.

It happened before Jack existed, yet he knew the story by heart. How young Ernie took a dare from his three older brothers. How he stole a leaky boat from a pond upstream. How he dragged it down to the river and launched it from an eddy. How his brothers egged him on, never foreseeing the possibility that Ernie was really that stupid or that eager to earn their respect. How Ernie rowed out to the middle in easy water, then stood up in the boat to deliver a mock military salute to the rapids ahead, then smiled back to his brothers. How the older boys began yelling at their kid brother to row back because the water was about to take off. How Ernie actually rowed downstream. How he guided the unworthy craft through the first set of kinetic rapids with surprising skill and accuracy. How the river then shot Ernie hard to the left in a huge sweeping turn, setting him up for a right-hand turn and a fast run at the narrows. How Ernie's mastery of whitewater petered out quickly. How the bow of the rowboat crashed headlong into the forbidding rock wall, spinning wildly out of control. How the stern of the boat caught the opposite rocky shore, causing Ernie to lose his useless oars and throwing him far from his natural center of gravity. How the upstream gunwale dipped down to take a deadly gulp from the river. How the whole thing flipped, sending Ernie into the river with the last bit of air he'd ever get.

They figure Ernie to be one of the few people ever to see what the river looks like beneath the surface at the Narrows. They figure he lived long enough to see something down there, because when his body finally bobbed up a half a mile downstream, it showed no signs of damage. No gashes. No broken bones. Nothing. Ernie was just wet and dead. The way Jack's dad told it, Ernie's dreadful death made the surviving Fish boys just that much wilder.

"A person can see a lot of trouble from up here," whispered Jack to the canyon.

"The way I see it, this is a pretty good place for a person to avoid trouble," she said to announce her return.

"Why can't you just leave me alone?"

"Hey. You're the one who brought me here. You can't have your cake and—"

"Eat this," he said as he displayed his middle finger. "And stop trying to tell me what I can and can't have."

"Aww, now that's more like it, Jack. Showin' a little spunk. Kickin' the draft open on the fire."

"Listen, why don't you just bundle up your patronizing sarcasm and get the hell off my rock."

"Believe you me, this is no treat for Yours Truly. I'd rather be anywhere but here, 'cause whenever I'm here I don't fare so well."

"You hold your own."

"I sure as shit try to, Jack. But let's not forget, this is your imagination at work here. You're calling the shots, so I can't win. On the other hand, neither can you, so long as you keep wasting your time with arguments that only happen in your head."

"Do me a big favor, okay? Go straight to hell. Do not pass go. Do not collect two hundred dollars."

"Why Jack!" she said with false astonishment. "You condemn me with a boring cliché? And I thought you loved me."

"Yeah, well I thought so, too. But what if I don't? What if I never did? What if I just thought I did, and then I played along from there because I didn't know what the hell I could do about it? How'd ya like that? Huh?"

"Well," she said, absorbing his assertion.

"Well hell, twenty-watt! You think this has been easy for me? You think I like this? Well I don't. Not one goddamn bit. And let me tell you something else, this whole mess has completely compromised my plans. And it makes me wish I'd never fallen for you in the first place, 'cause it's just not helping."

"Oh, so you DO love me."

"I don't know if I do or if I don't. All I know for sure is I'd rather not."

"Listen, Jack. You don't need a big degree to understand that nobody controls who they love. So if you really don't love me, I guess I can understand that."

"Thank you."

"You're welcome. But the thing that really bugs me about all of this is the way you're treating me, Jack. I just don't think I deserve it. After all, I've done a lot for you. I've been real good to you. And, I let you get acquainted with the pleasures of the bedroom when a lot of guys that age are still dating their Playboys."

"Okay. Fine. You introduced me to the wonderful world of fornication. Thanks, again. I'll be forever in your debt. Can't begin to describe my gratitude. Of course."

"You're welcome again," she said.

"Okay. But that only gets us so far down the road, doesn't it. There's more to me than that. There's more to life than that, and I wanna go find out what the hell that's all about. I've got to. And I can't do it with you, because you're not curious enough, or smart enough, or ambitious enough or even mature enough."

"Well I'll be. There it is at last."

"There what is?"

"The truth, handsome Jack. The goddamnmotherfuckinson ofbitchin truth."

Jack absorbed her comment without making a sound.

"That's right," she said with a confident chuckle.

"Huh," said Jack, trying to get his hands around the idea.

"Ya know, Jack. If I were a more insightful person, I'd say you're in the process of having one of those epiphanies. But Lord knows, I wouldn't use a big word like that on my own. Appreciate you sharin' your vocabulary with me here today."

A wall of colder wind moved across the canyon toward Jack, reaching him just as he was about to tell her something that seemed significant. But the wind blew the thought away.

"Can I go now?" she asked with an impish tone. I mean, are we through here for now? Because it seems to me that maybe we just hit on something, and that maybe you need a little time to be by yourself. After all, Jack, that's what this place is for, right? So maybe I'll just be on my way. Leave you be. And then, if you like, we can put a finish on this conversation somewhere else.

Maybe some place where I can be a whole person. 'Cause like I say, I never come out right when you conjure me up this way. And not only is it unfair to me, it's unfair to you. Think about that, okay, Jack? And just remember this: whatever you decide to do about us, it'll be all right. Honest. Just so long as you're brave enough to honor your own truth. Okay? Okay, then. I'll be going."

Gray and green surrounded Jack as he sat there on the moss at the edge of the Camp of the Gods. Nearly all other colors had disappeared, giving way to those two colors as the afternoon began surrendering to an early nightfall. Green trees near and far. Gray rocks large and small. Green moss old and new. Gray bark smooth and craggy. Green river calm and torrid. And overriding all of it, homogenous white-gray clouds.

They were pressing in hard on Jack, lowering by the minute, seamlessly shrouding the mountains. Taking over. But Jack didn't fully notice at first, because he was consumed by what she'd said, and because it always took him a while to get comfortable with an idea that wasn't his.

The wind finally got his attention, though. It snapped him to, and made him look up.

The whiteness was coming.

It came from the direction of the highest mountain across the canyon, Rocky Top. It was spreading out in slow motion, broadening its reach east and west of the peak, creeping down the southern slopes, filling the basin at the base of the mountain, rolling emphatically toward Jack. It transfixed him, just as her words had done a few minutes earlier. He couldn't look away.

Jack knew what it was. He'd seen it before. But he'd never seen it quite this way. And it frightened him in a way he could not have anticipated. Jack felt alone and exposed, and he wanted to run. But he could not move.

It pointed Jack out from high across the canyon. It bore down on him. It took aim at him, seeming to recognize him, pondering for a moment what to do about him. It pressed on in, making Jack feel small and weak and helpless, making him think of his mother.

It got bigger.

Wider.

Taller.

Closer.

Whiter.

Jack's mouth was open. He could hear the sound of his own heart, pounding loudly, echoing up out of his throat, like a miner tapping out distress signals on a wheelbarrow as he lay dying deep in a shaft. The desperate sound of absolute aloneness, which is nothing at all like solitude.

Everything else, though, was getting quiet. The wind was silent. The river below kept roaring through the narrows, but that roar was now muffled.

There was just the massive choreography of approaching weather.

More coldness now.

A sharp, tingly shiver emerged between Jack's shoulder blades that surged up his spine to the back of his neck, spilling out in a wash over the tops of his shoulders and then half way down his arms. Prickly hot and cold. His neck twitched his head hard to the left, reflexively. Jack suddenly sucked in an immense, overdue breath. Letting it out, he realized that the shiver had made it all the way down to the backs of his hands. His eyes were drying, not having blinked for an age.

The foreboding force came right at Jack.

The damn thing is drawing a bead on my forehead, he thought. *I know what it is,* he thought again. *I know what's going on. It's time for a reckoning. It's my own personal come-to-Jesus meeting. Time to get square with the carpenter's old man,* he thought. *Time to get my ass kicked for being such a self-indulgent jerk. Time to learn what's what and who's who in the here and now. Okay. I understand. No place to hide now. No way to avoid the truth. Well, goddamn it, bring it on. What the hell! Let me have it. I know I've been a shit. I know I deserve whatever's comin'.*

Jack did not look away.

And in the very next instant, he was suddenly and overwhelmingly rewarded for his courage. Alone on his mossy rock, Jack had faced up to everything. And in doing so, everything changed. Fear gave way to focus. Depression gave way to wonder. Confusion gave way to clarity. Because he had drawn a bead on that which dogged him, vanquishing it.

The legions swarmed in toward him. Too many to imagine or count. A conquering army charging in at a steep angle, glistening bayonets fixed, full force, beyond the point of no return. Jack could see them more clearly, and the enormous anticipation of it all sent shock wave after joyous shock wave out from between his shoulder blades, rolling again and again out to his extremities. His elbows and knees all but ached with eagerness. His ribs tightened. His fingers flexed and splayed repeatedly, nervously happy. Ready.

Then, out in front of the others, Jack saw the scout approaching. The point of the attack. Closer and closer. Jack locked in on it. Braced himself, knowing exactly what to do. Jack smiled broadly. Then he opened his mouth wide to take communion.

The first snowflake flew right in.

Jack had been saved from himself. Again. And though it took him a good long while to recognize the truth of what was happening to him, he had indeed rediscovered the thing that is always lurking somewhere around the Camp of the Gods—a measure of personal peace.

Minutes later, Jack and the moss and the rocks and the manzanitas were white with snow. His world was reborn. And Jack felt grateful, because the thing he'd been afraid of was ultimately the thing he valued most. He felt it was a gift. And he felt foolish that it had to be given to him over and over again. But Jack understood how it works, at least for him: that he had to keep relearning certain lessons. And that over time, more and more of it would stick like snow on the manzanitas.

He resolved to put it right with her. And with that resolution tucked firmly away for future use, he turned away from the edge that overlooked the now invisible river. He retraced his steps through the camp, and then down the trail through the woods, heading for home. The descending darkness posed no challenge, because he was buoyed by once again seeing the light of day.

Your secrets are safe.

That's what the falling snow seemed to be saying as flakes kissed his face.

Under the Apples and Stars

The dance floor Old Man Flores built was down in his pasture, in among the apple trees his grandfather planted beside the creek. You had to drive down the lane Mr. Flores shared with his neighbors to get there, back about a quarter mile from the main road. The tall grass of summer crowded in on both sides of the gravel lane, making it feel even narrower. But then you'd pass through the gate Mr. Flores left open into his pasture, which was green from irrigation and trimmed neat and low by his cattle and sheep. That's where everything opened up and got beautiful.

I remember going to see Mr. and Mrs. Flores long before we started dancing in their orchard. My father took me there when I was a little girl, to buy fresh milk and sometimes eggs if they had any brown ones. They were a talkative pair, the Flores. My folks liked them a lot, and father always cautioned me not to say anything about how short they were.

My mother told me Mrs. Flores got the idea about making money from an outdoor dance floor from an article in *Collier's* magazine. Mother said Mr. Flores grumbled around his barnyard for weeks after it first came up, kicking at dried cowpies, cursing in Spanish, and complaining to his animals that it would be expensive to build a good dance floor and that nobody would show up with their money. And if they did, he further complained, he'd have to stay up past his normal bedtime just to keep an eye on things.

Mrs. Flores prevailed, which according to my mother she almost always did. A sweet but persistent lady, said Mother.

Mr. Flores had several practical skills. And if his dance floor was any indication, carpentry must have been one of his best. Because he constructed something fine using the best local cedar. Word spread fast around the North Santiam Canyon about that new attraction, and the Flores' dance floor was crowded on its very first night.

That was in 1932, just seven years after they built the steel railroad bridge in Mill City. I was sixteen years old and shy about my height, because at five foot ten I was taller than a good many boys. Still I loved to dance, and all of my friends were planning to show up. I was easily persuaded to join in.

It was a Saturday in early August. I remember because it was the time of the meteor showers. Seven of us crowded onto the pickup belonging to one of the dads, and we rolled down the lane past the Flores place about eight o'clock. Mr. Flores was there at the gate, wearing a bright plaid shirt under his overalls, directing people where and how to park. This was across the creek from the orchard, and we used Mr. Flores' bouncy footbridge to reach the other side.

And there it was—Mr. Flores' unpainted dance palace: an elevated wood floor that looked to be about twenty-five feet wide and maybe forty feet long. We had to climb up four steps just to set foot on the main floor. He'd built a railing that went all the way around, with a nice, wide board as the top rail, which was ideal for leaning or parking your refreshment while dancing. Every third post extended upward a good four feet above the top rail. And at the top of each tall post was a kerosene lantern hanging from a wooden peg. There were benches, too. Simple wooden benches like you'd find on anybody's back porch. They surrounded the floor on three sides. The end without benches was where the band set up.

He charged us twenty cents each, but that didn't stop Mr. Flores' dance floor from being a quick success. Boys and girls, men and women, they came from all around. And I somehow managed to save enough money to go every single Saturday night until school started. I was quite a dancing fiend back then, not that anybody would know it today. Everyone said I was good, too. I'm not sure that was the truth, but all I cared about was having fun. Even if it meant getting eaten by mosquitoes, or dancing with my girlfriends when there weren't enough boys to go around. That was the one place I could go, the one thing I could do, that made me forget about my troubles. Because when the music was playing and the dance floor was full of motion and smiles, it was my elixir. I've known many kinds of happiness in my time, but I can't recall one that topped a Saturday night at the Flores'.

The last dance that summer was set for Labor Day Weekend. Word got out that Mrs. Flores convinced her husband to pay the extra expense of hiring a seven-piece band out of Eugene. One that normally only played on the university campus, at functions and affairs the likes of which I could only imagine.

I had a big decision to make. Would I wear the same outfit I'd worn every other Saturday night? Or would I risk wearing my one new dress, which my mother made specifically for the new school year? The same dilemma applied to my shoes. Wear the old ones, which could no longer be tricked into looking good? Or wear my brand new oxford lace-ups, with their rich, brown leather and their baseball-style stitching?

The responsible thing would have been to save the new stuff for school, keeping in mind how long they'd have to last me. But I had a special feeling about that last dance. Like something good was going to happen. Like there was a reason to make an extra effort. Like whatever it was, it might be worth getting my mother angry with me.

I stood there, looking closely at me and my brown hair in the full-length mirror, trying to decide if I actually needed the benefit of a new outfit. I looked at my nose, which has always been a bit larger than I'd like. I studied my small smile, which I've always been told has a certain charm, even today. I looked straight into my own brown eyes, trying to imagine how I might appear to someone else if I sent them an honest gaze. I followed the gentle arch of my eyebrows, and judged them to be one of my finest features. Then I stood back from the mirror. And in doing so, I was reminded of my height….

I wore the new stuff, of course. It was years later that I learned my mother actually hoped I'd dress my best that night, because she too had had a premonition about the dance, and it made her hopeful for my future.

We arrived a little later than usual at Mr. Flores', and we were shocked to learn that because of the out of town band, his admission had gone up a nickel. The parking area was much fuller than normal, and there were several cars that none of us recognized. Must be friends of the band, we said to one another.

It was mostly dark already, as the sun had been setting earlier and earlier like it always does that time of year. The kerosene lanterns were putting out a wonderful, warm glow as we approached the dance floor after crossing the bouncy footbridge. We could see lots of people. Many more than ever before. And the floor looked dangerously overcrowded, which only fired our excitement.

The band from Eugene was louder than any other band that summer. They played with an energy we had not heard before. The music seemed to be echoing off of the apple trees, and the sloping, green pasture, and the back of Mr. Flores' barn and outbuildings, and off of the walls of the canyon itself.

Climbing the four steps up to the platform, I was pleased to discover that every member of the band was a Negro. I'd never seen a Negro before that night.

The very moment I stepped onto the dance floor, a young man I didn't know asked me to dance. I opened my mouth to say something about needing to settle in first, but that hesitant sound I made was completely drowned out by the music and commotion. And before I could get my mouth closed again, I'd already been danced right into the middle of the pack. I didn't mind one bit.

Six or seven songs went by before I began making my way back to the railing. And in that brief flash of time I got asked to dance by a number of boys. Not one of them was familiar to me, and I didn't care, because everyone looked good that night.

There was no moon. The stars that were visible between the treetops of Mr. Flores' orchard were the most brilliant kind. Leaning on the rail and looking up to the northern sky, I saw a lone meteor streak from the top of one tree to the top of another. I imagined its purpose was to connect one apple to another, and somehow that made the evening just that much more magical.

I turned back to the dance floor and instantly felt myself becoming more keenly aware of that magic, more attuned to the rhythm and mood of that outdoor room, more appreciative of the energy. I felt as though I understood what was happening just a little better than anyone else out there under the apples and stars. I felt serene, comforted, and at peace.

There was a sudden tingling at the base of my neck that sent a shockwave throughout my body, erupting in goose bumps down the length of my arms and the backs of my legs. I wondered if anyone noticed. But how could they?

My breathing became shallow and rapid. My eyes wouldn't focus. The people and the music and the lanterns and the trees and the stars, they all became one swirling, mesmerizing rush of color and texture and sound. I felt myself smiling. I felt an overwhelming need to share what I was sensing. What I was witness to. The happiness. The impossibility of anything going wrong, and the certainty of things going right. Only good could come. Only I could accept and embrace it. Only in that perfect blur of a moment.

The chaos of people dancing suddenly took on an order. Where once there was a wiggly-waggly mishmash of arms and legs and heads, there came a pattern. A system. An intent. Like crops in rows, or geese in flight. And right through the middle of it all, a kind of corridor emerged. A path. A clean, straight line that connected the spot where I stood to the spot where I had to go. To the opposite corner of the dance floor. To the railing. To the center point between two of Mr. Flores' brightest lanterns. The warm, yellow light showed me the way. And it showed that someone was there waiting for me. A young man. Someone who knew nothing of me or what I was feeling and seeing. A young man with his angular back to the dance floor, with his elbows on the corner railing, with his eyes obviously fixed on something off in the darkness, looking comfortable in his detachment.

I moved toward the corner, down that path, unafraid.

The dancers closed behind me, funneling me into the corner where the railings converged on the man. A slight breeze moved the air in front of me, carrying the scent of ripening apples and giving me even more confidence; a clearing breath. As I stepped into speaking range, nearly touching range, the young man turned to me.

He was nearly six feet tall, lean top to bottom, and muscular in a way that was more about hard work than anything else.

He cleaned up nicely, though. He knew how to dress himself like it actually mattered. Black shoes so shiny they reflected the dim lantern light. Gray slacks pressed with a precision that would impress even the most judgmental parents. Thin, blue suspenders with silver clasps; two dark stripes running straight over his flat, efficient torso, providing a vivid contrast to his church-white shirt, which was also pressed as if someone's life depended on it. The collar opened wide at the neck and rested comfortably on his collarbones, the way maple leaves look in late summer, impressive but relaxed. He wore a hat, unlike every other fellow on the dance floor that night—a mouse-gray fedora with a nice broad brim, a gray satin band, and two oval indentations on the front of the crown.

That young man was clearly not one to tan easily. Being the end of summer and all, you'd expect everyone to have a little color on their face. But his had a happy kind of pink to it. A healthy sort of pale. With an unmistakable but natural blush on his cheeks.

He smiled at me, and those cheeks came to attention, becoming round and contoured in a way that made me want to touch them. His smile was flat and broad. And even though his lips were thin, I found myself liking his look. I certainly liked his eyes, because each of them smiled on their own, which made him something of a threat to my better judgment.

"What are you looking at out there in the darkness?" I asked.

"Well I'll be. So you've been watching me," said the young man with a playful tone.

"Not at all."

"Not at all, she says."

"That's right, not at all. But the question still stands."

"Listen, I'm just not that good at small talk, so you might be barkin' up the wrong tree here," he said with a body language that contradicted his words.

"I've not barked even once, but I do have another question for you."

He raised his eyebrows in anticipation.

"Why don't you ask me to dance?"

"I'm not much for dancing either."

"Hmm," I said with sarcasm. "He doesn't like small talk. He doesn't dance. Makes me wonder why he bothered to show up at all. Maybe he's too good for all of this common fun."

"You want to dance?"

"Well of course I do," I replied with an air of success.

"Well tell ya what. You go on and dance to your little heart's content, because there's sure a bunch of fellas here who'll gladly help you out. And then, when you're done dancin', and if I'm still standing here in my corner, you can just make your way back on over here."

"Give me one good reason why I should," I said with as much defiance as I could manage under the circumstances."

"One good reason?"

"Just one."

"Okay, then. Try this one: maybe by then I'll be of a mind to tell you what it is I've been lookin' at out there tonight."

That tore it for me. I spun on my heels and shot right back into the crowded dance floor. And sure enough, another young man asked me to dance. And I saw it as a salvation, because the last thing I wanted was for that intriguing fellow with the blue suspenders to see me make it to the other side of the dance floor without attracting a partner. I needed that kind of immediate success, because in my heart of hearts, I knew I'd be back in his corner before long.

And I was.

I'm an old woman now, alone for the most part. I keep his ashes in an old cookie jar that sits at the back of the top shelf in my bedroom closet. The jar is ceramic, done in a shade of buttermilk yellow. It's decorated with red apples and green leaves. It was a wedding gift from Mr. and Mrs. Flores, both of whom bragged for years that if not for their dance floor in the orchard, my young man and I would never have met. Would never have married.

My husband and I always allowed that the Flores were correct, and that there was something very special about that place and time. We remembered it together for sixty-three years, and we spoke of it often on warm summer evenings. We'd both smile at the memory. I'd smile my little smile. And he'd smile his.

It was a smile that often came with a little-boy twinkle in his sweet, squinty eyes. The way apple pie sometimes comes with ice cream.

Yes, he did indeed tell me what he was looking at out in the darkness the night we met. But it turned out he wasn't looking at anything in particular, because he was actually wrestling with a kind of assignment he'd given himself:

"What to say to the devil," he told me.

I found out later that he'd been chewing on that one for years, figuring all along that he'd surely go to Hell one day for who he was and how he lived. The course of his life changed that night, though, and I maybe had something to do with making sure he'd never need that kind of opening line.

PART TWO

People Cuss the Crows

Buying the Flying A station had been a big decision for Roy. There was nothing to pumping gas and checking oil, but the prospect of running any sort of business was a big deal. Cathy said she'd keep the books and mind the money. She was five years older, and her confidence cinched it for him. That, and the look in her serene brown eyes, confirming the wisdom of the decision. The seller was dying of lung cancer and let the Larimers have it on a friendly contract. Almost nothing down and an easy monthly to the seller's soon-to-be widow. They hadn't been at it long when Cathy told Roy over supper that she'd figured out why the previous owners never got ahead. "Pumping doesn't pay," she said. "We've got to find ways to supplement."

By the time they got to the pie that evening, the plan was set for them to buy a used wrecker. It turned out to have been a good idea, because on that very night, the only other guy running a tow truck in the entire North Santiam Canyon took off with his wife's younger sister. This created two canyon scandals, the greater of which was the loss of a good wrecker service. Roy Larimer came to the rescue.

Roy was not an attractive man. He knew it and accepted it. His round face. His uneven brow. His big rubbery ears. His receding hair. His inability to keep his brown plastic glasses sitting squarely on the bridge of his broad nose. Consequently, Roy set his sights low in life, figuring that so long as he could get someone to marry him, and then stay with him for the raising of the children, that that would probably be enough. He never counted on a pretty wife, let alone one so full of insight and praise and understanding. He told himself that Cathy was his prize for not being a creep. But he could never truly get his hands around the equation that allowed him to marry as well as he had. Like maybe it was an oversight, and that someone or something would eventually come along to right the wrong. Until then, he figured, it's probably best not to let on to anyone how undeserving he felt. That might jinx it. That might prompt everybody he ever knew to stand up and say, *We thought so, too. So why don't you just give it up, Roy Larimer, and let the poor woman alone so she can go find a man who is worthy.*

Roy was lonely in a way that no one could see. Because he hadn't had a true friend since the eighth grade, when Ernie Fish drowned. Roy got stuck after that. And things stayed that way all through high school, and then in the army, and then in the workaday life that followed. There was a time when it seemed like he might become buddies with a couple of fellows who often came in together for a Saturday morning fill-up: George Howard and Ivan Thrower, good friends and hunting partners who were friendly to Roy. They joked around a lot, and it always seemed as though they were about to do something fun. Like gold panning. Or gray digger hunting. Or poking around one of the old, forgotten logging camps up in the foothills. It started to seem as though they might invite Roy to come along. Roy imagined them asking him to shut down the Flying A for the rest of the day, so he could go play. But they never did. And Roy's fantasies of friendship were ultimately destroyed by one incident at the pump:

George and Ivan were getting gas, sitting inside the cab of George's pickup, and bragging about the one thing each man had going for himself. George described himself as a keen judge of character. Ivan went on about how he could read an entire issue of *Mechanix Illustrated* without being stumped by a single word. Then Roy made the mistake of leaning into the conversation and foolishly offering that his strength was in marrying well. This seriousness was too much for Ivan, whose lightning-quick retort was to suggest that in Roy's case, it was dumb luck and nothing more. Ivan was smiling when he said it, but the insult was landed. The wound was open. And the salt came in the form of one final comment from Ivan, about how he wouldn't mind hanging his britches on Cathy Larimer's bedpost just once, so she'd know just how poorly she'd married. George and Ivan kept coming back to the Flying A after that, but Roy no longer spoke to them. And he began wondering if Cathy knew Ivan.

People cuss the crows. But Roy Larimer had been particularly fond of them since he was a boy. Not so much when they're all sitting up in the treetops and cawing at each other, although Roy sometimes found that to be as amusing as it was loud. Mostly, it was the way they flew silently back into the woods at the end of a hot summer day. The way they head for the hills in crude formation, but with lots of intent. Riding high between the canyon walls on the last fading thermals of the day, as if they'd punched out from work and were heading back for a nice, quiet evening at home with the family, the day's cawing behind them. The thought of it made Roy feel good about things. Because he figured that if such simplicity was good enough for the crows, then it damn sure ought to be good enough for the likes of him. The crows are unappreciated and misunderstood, Roy realized, but they've got the big things in life figured out about right. And he figured to follow them back into the trees every day.

The Lake Dog

Cathy and their four kids were heavy sleepers. Roy went the other way, always stirring at the slightest sound and then listening to make sure it didn't repeat. When the phone rang just after midnight, it was an explosion in his ears. A towing call from the police dispatcher.

"A wreck up the highway, by the lake," the dispatcher said into Roy's ear. "A bad one. Look for Deputy Davis."

Cathy sighed a small smile in the darkness when Roy kissed her forehead to say good-bye.

"Back when I'm able," he whispered.

He pulled the wrecker onto the midnight highway and flipped on his red overheads, always his favorite part of any run. The boy in him celebrated how the piercing red beams rotated around him as he drove, catching and reflecting off of anything that was white or shiny on the roadside. It's not something he ever talked about. He savored it like a secret piece of hard candy. But the sweetness and flavor was always all but gone by the time he arrived on scene.

Just past milepost 73. That's what the dispatcher had said on the phone. Where the road takes a hard left as you're heading east. Roy knew the spot well from a wreck three years before. Some kids from Detroit hit a rock in the road that nearly put them into the lake. Nobody got hurt that time. But their pickup took out the guardrail and ended up with one wheel hanging over the edge. Roy had winched it back to safety and life went on for the boys, who never seemed to understand how close a call they'd had. Roy knew, but it wasn't his place to say.

Pulling up at nearly 1:00 a.m., Roy was surprised to discover so little commotion. Just Mike Davis and his county squad car, and five red flares on the pavement. Normally there'd be chaos. And gawkers. But not this time, and it seemed weird.

"Mike," said Roy as a greeting to the deputy.

"Sorry to roust you, Roy."

"Gotta pay the bills like everyone else," said Roy. "Besides, looks like the reinforcements are a little slow tonight."

"Stretched thin again. But then, there's no real rush on this one."

"No survivors?"

"Three dead. Single car. Right over the edge."

"Christ!"

"Yeah."

"They said it was a bad one, but it's been a while since we lost three," said Roy.

"Yeah, I guess they won't mind being crowded in the ambulance when it gets here."

"I guess."

"They were drinking, of course."

"Of course," said Roy.

"Well, at least they didn't make it all the way down to the lake tonight. That woulda made things a whole lot worse. For us, I mean."

"How far down?" asked Roy.

"Eighty feet, give or take. A stump stopped 'em."

"Are we solid against that stump? No chance it's gonna take off again?" asked Roy.

"Seems dead solid."

Roy was glad for the darkness on wrecks like this. It gave him something of a choice about what he actually had to see, because he could aim his three-cell flashlight as he saw fit, focusing the beam on where and how to hook his line to the vehicle, and avoiding as best he could the sight of blood, suffering, and death.

The plan was for Roy to work his way down the slope to where the car came to rest against the stump, then set a line on the lower end of the wreck to remove any chance of further descent, and then climb up out of there to tend his tow truck. With that accomplished, Deputy Davis could safely lead the effort to retrieve the three bodies, aided by the five volunteer firemen who finally showed up with the ambulance.

"Any idea who he is?" asked Roy of the men hauling the first body back up to the highway.

"We ain't gotten around to checking his wallet yet, Roy Boy," said Andy Sawyer, a former Navy boxer who disliked being asked. Roy felt stupid for not having given Andy a chance to catch his breath, and he instantly hoped the exchange wouldn't stop Andy and his wife, Maxine, from gassing up at the Flying A.

"I don't recognize him," offered the second volunteer fireman, who Roy recognized as Kenny Hoyle, chief of the volunteers. "But hell, Roy. He's so boogered up, I doubt his own mother would know him."

"There it is," said Roy. "Gonna be any trouble getting the other two out?"

"Looks to be a pretty clean deal," said the serious but affable Kenny Hoyle.

"That's good," said Roy.

Next up the hill was the small body of a woman with no shoes. Roy saw her long brown hair in the headlights and thought maybe it was someone he'd sold gas to at one time or another. But she, too, was in a bad way, and unrecognizable. Roy wondered if she had been attractive before the wreck.

"It's a damn shame," said Roy to the third and fourth huffing firemen who served as her escorts, and who were unfamiliar to Roy.

"Always is," said the older fireman.

The younger fireman did not speak, and it appeared to Roy that it was all the young man could do to not throw up. Roy shared a glance with the older one that intimated an understanding of the young fireman's plight. That it's rough the first few times you pull a body out. That it takes a bit of getting used to. That a person might never get used to it.

"One more, I guess," said Roy.

"Yep," answered the older fireman. "The deputy and our driver are bringing him up. Then we'll be on our way."

"And maybe you'll be back home in bed before the missus misses you," offered Roy.

The comment caught the older fireman off guard, and then prompted a sarcastic grin.

"I guess you've never seen my wife, have you, mister?"

"The only way I'd know her is if she bought gas at the Flying A," said Roy.

"Larimer, isn't it?"

"Roy Larimer."

"Well, she prefers the Chevron station up on the highway. Which means you pro'bly never seen her. So take my word, Larimer. Ain't no reason to rush home."

Roy had no idea how to respond to the older fireman's candor, but his facial expression said something innocuous like, *Well I'll be....*

The third body was that of a man known to all the rescuers. Pike Early was the picture of serenity on the stretcher, because there was no disfigurement or blood. Just the neutral expression of sudden death.

"Poor sonofabitch," said Kenny Hoyle from the darkness.

"Yeah, well, ol' Early may have been a sonofabitch," said Andy Sawyer. "But he didn't die poor. Not when you take into account how many twenties I left behind in that damn tavern of his."

Everyone laughed in acknowledgement of The Narrows Tavern.

"He was never popular with the church folk, was he?" offered the older fireman in search of confirmation.

"Nope," answered Deputy Davis. "But you know how it is, boys. Some of us are meant for pews, and some of us are meant for bar stools. And rare is the man who sits comfortably on both."

"So how do ya figure Pike ended up with these other two?" asked Roy. "These strangers, I mean."

"Oh who the hell cares?" shot back the cranky Andy Sawyer. "Jesus, Larimer! Why do you ask such stupid ass questions anyway? Nobody gives a shit, ya big dummy."

The rescuers quietly ignored the outburst of their irritable comrade, who shuffled off into the darkness to pee. Roy's face showed no response, as had become his defensive custom. Then Deputy Davis refocused the group by providing some context to the accident.

"Here's how it looks to me, boys. They were heading east. Traveling way too fast. And judging by the all the stubbies I found in the car and on the slope, and the smell of things, it's pretty clear they were having themselves a party on wheels."

The rescuers nodded their comprehension.

"So they came up to this curve right here," continued Deputy Davis. "And they were probably gonna be okay, even with all that speed and all that beer. But then something got in the way."

"We didn't see where any rocks came down off the hill," interjected Kenny Hoyle. "Most times it's a rock in the road."

"Most times, yes," echoed the deputy.

"What the hell?" pressed the older fireman.

"Bear," answered Deputy Davis. "They damn near hit a black bear in the road."

"Well I'll be goddamned," said the older fireman.

"No shit. A bear?" pressed Roy.

"That's my theory, boys," continued the deputy. "I was poking around with my flashlight before any of you got here, and I found fresh bear sign right over there."

The deputy pointed to the opposite side of the highway, where the soft dirt of the uphill embankment came down to the ditch where water flowed year-round.

"Big pads and long claws, right there in the dirt," said Deputy Davis. "Plain as day. And then we've got these skid marks here, which tells me they hit the brakes."

"Well I'll be goddamned," said the fireman who'd uttered the same words just moments before.

"So you figure the bear walked out in front of 'em, do ya?" asked Roy.

"Copy that."

"And you figure the driver, whoever it was, musta swerved to miss the bear," said Kenny Hoyle.

"And here we all are, being brought up to trust our instincts, as if that's always the best way," observed Deputy Davis.

"Sure wasn't the best way tonight. Least not for these guys," said the youngest fireman, who'd finally found his voice.

The observation was welcomed by all, because it meant the young fireman was beginning to collect his wits. Yet it all but stopped the conversation in its tracks, leaving nothing but the sound of three engines idling in the night: the police car, the ambulance, and Roy's wrecker.

"Okay, boys," said the deputy. "Let's see about getting this over and done with, shall we? Take our friends on down to the hospital in Stayton. I'll start my paperwork and put out some fresh flares. Roy, you go ahead and see if that car's gonna come up out of there tonight. Hate to have to come back here in the daylight to finish up."

With that, Roy broke off from the group and began descending back down the embankment, making his way to the car.

He scanned the beam of his flashlight up and down the wreck, concluding there was a reasonable chance of getting it up and out in one clean shot. If he hooked it up just so. If he lined up the wrecker just right. He took his time to think it through, realizing there was no urgency. Just a tricky job that needed to be done well.

He was struck by how peaceful it was there above the lake at what was now 3:00 a.m. How quiet it was. And though there was no wind, Roy could feel the air moving in glacial chunks, massive and slow, but not cold. Cool at best. Invigorating.

Roy thought about how odd it was to be out there doing such an unsavory task, and to be feeling such an untimely sense of wonder at his surroundings. Three people just died at that very spot. But all he could think about was how lucky he was to even be there. Just another thing he could never speak of, he figured. Because people would have yet another reason to think of him as weird. Maybe Cathy would understand. Maybe not.

A dog barked from far across the lake, clear over on the other side, where the blackness knew no limit. The sound seemed to fit the scene, Roy thought. He sensed near perfection in the way the bark punctuated the stillness. The way it snapped him to attention, and caused him to turn his head instinctively toward the source. He felt animal-like. Raw and alert. Ready to devour the mysteries of the small hours without fear or apprehension. Vital as hell. All five senses screaming with curiosity.

The dog barked again, only this time it sounded different. Closer than before, perhaps. Something.

Again the lake dog barked. And once again, the quality of the sound changed. Now it seemed more desperate and distressed. The dog was not barking its awareness of something in the night. It was barking a plea. *A call for help*, Roy thought. It made him wish he could do something. Or at least understand what was going on over there. It was just a feeling he had, standing there with flashlight in hand beside the wreck in the dark. *Stupid dog.*

"Get to work, Roy," he said out loud.

Roy maneuvered his way to the front bumper, figuring that if he pulled from that end, he stood the best chance of getting the car aligned to come up the slope before it became fully dislodged from the sturdy stump.

He put his flashlight on the ground so it could shine its beam up under the car, freeing both hands to rehook the line to the undercarriage. His gear clanged against the metal parts, partially masking yet another bark from the lake dog in the distance. Trouble was, the bark now sounded disturbingly close. So much so that a shiver shot up Roy's spine and directly into the fleshy folds on the back of his neck. He stopped working. He stopped breathing. He listened.

The sound came again. And this time, the shivers fired across Roy's shoulders and then down the skin that covered his triceps, right to the elbows.

It was not a bark at all, Roy realized. He was wrong about there being a dog somewhere in the distance and the dark.

Rather, it was a voice.

A human voice.

Not a voice saying something, but one simply trying to make a sound. Roy grabbed his flashlight and stood up sharply, and then spoke to defend himself.

"Who's out there?" he said in a big voice. "What the hell you doin' down here? Speak up now!"

There was no reply. And even if there had been one at that moment, Roy would've struggled to hear it over his own labored breathing. His flashlight fired a probing beam across the steep slope in search of the source. And in the middle of this disorienting moment, Roy's mind said something about how he wished the sound had remained a dog across the lake, because that would have made more sense. But dogs just don't sound like that. Then Roy thought about trying to get the deputy's attention, so he wouldn't be the only one trying to figure things out.

"But what the hell would I say without looking like a fool?" he said out loud. "I thought it was a dog but now I don't? Idiot."

The voice came again. Definitely from somewhere down the slope, and a little to the left. And this time there were words.

The table.... Roy thought he heard.

"HELLO?" shouted Roy.

"Lori. Set the table," said the voice.

It was a woman's voice. And in the next instant, Roy drew a bead on a precise direction, down and to the left as he'd previously thought. The flashlight let his eyes see a sun-bleached stump that matched the direction. Roy moved toward it, lowering himself cautiously down the slope over the loose, noisy rocks.

He alternated between shining the light on the stump and then where he was walking. The dancing light skipped across something bright red. Something on a bush that was dead ahead. A piece of cloth.

When he got to it, Roy picked up what appeared to be a woman's shirt. In red bandana material.

"Do as I ask, Lori," said the woman's voice.

Roy aimed his flashlight directly at the stump, and that's when something brilliant reflected right back at him. The full intensity of his three-cell flashlight seemed to explode with a precise, pinpoint burst of light, just in front of the stump. The sight of it frightened Roy, but he went to it anyway.

A sparkling earring.

Mary Soderberg collected the complete set of eight smoke-colored tumblers Roy had been giving away at the Flying A. One free with each fillup. That's the very first thing he thought after realizing who it was and what must have happened to the middle school math teacher.

"Lori done yet?" she asked Roy, who realized that Lori was Mary's teenage daughter.

"Mary?"

"Supper's ready. Tired a waitin' on that girl."

"Mary, it's Roy from the Flying A. Mary?"

"Roy. Staying for supper? Casserole."

"Mary, we're gonna have to get you up outta here. You understand?"

"Fine, Roy. Maybe wait 'til after supper."

The fourth victim of the crash seemed oddly comfortable to Roy. Even though she'd been thrown from the car. Even though she'd been broken in many ways. Even though she'd been stripped of her red bandana shirt and left to lean against a stump wearing a big red bra.

"Listen, Mary. I'm gonna go get us some help now," said Roy. "It'll just take a few minutes, I promise. And then we'll see if we can't get you out of this mess."

"Do what you want. Like my husband," said Mary. "But if that casserole gets cold...."

Roy placed his flashlight on the stump above Mary's head and aimed it toward the slope so he could find her again.

"Okay, Mary. I'll be right back. You keep an eye on my flashlight for me."

"Casserole gets cold, hardly ever as good."

§

Hours later, Roy was back home in his own kitchen making coffee. His thick, grease-stained hands measured out quivering scoops from the Folgers can. Each scoop landed squarely in the basket of the electric percolator they got as a wedding gift. The lid with the glass globe snapped into place, making more noise than he liked. Roy much preferred the promising gurgle of the perk, which was no louder than usual. But this time it was enough to rouse Cathy into the kitchen, where she found Roy sitting in a daze. She poured herself a cup and sat down with him.

"Hi," she said softly.

Roy mustered a weak smile as her reward, looking his wife squarely in the eyes.

"Too soon to talk about it?" she asked.

"Yeah. No. I don't know."

"Hmm."

The two of them sat in silence for a moment, sipping coffee that was too hot for anything more aggressive. Then Cathy got up and left the room. Roy heard the toilet flush. She returned to her seat at the kitchen table.

"Milepost 73 by the lake. Bear in the road," said Roy. "Hasn't Lori Soderberg been over here for supper or something?"

"Not for supper, hon. But she came for a sleepover once. A bear?"

"That's right. Last Halloween," he said.

"God! Is that who it was last night? Lori Soderberg?!"

"You'd think it would be the kids out partying, wouldn't you?" said Roy. "But it was the grown-ups. Mary Soderberg, Pike Early, and a couple none of us knew. All dead."

"Oh, Roy!" Cathy said with a flash of compassion for her husband. "Did you have to—"

"I tried to stay out of the worst of it, you know? But when I found Mary, that really didn't work any more. They already took the three bodies from the car, and we didn't even know she was out there."

"You found her afterward?"

"Alive and talking."

"Oh, Roy!"

"Yeah, and I went for help. But by the time Mike Davis and I got back to her—"

"Goddamnit, Roy," said Cathy as she began to understand what he had been through.

Nothing else needed to be said for a few moments. Roy shifted forward onto his elbows, which were planted firmly onto the gray Formica of their dinette, anchoring his forearms, steadying the hot cup of coffee he held in two hands, just below his lips, in the sipping position. Cathy watched Roy without looking at him directly, trying not to fuss.

"You ever hear about any trouble in the Soderberg house?" asked Roy. "Between Lori's folks?"

"No," said Cathy. "But I've never been much for canyon gossip."

"Huh."

"What?"

"Oh, I'm thinking there must've been trouble," said Roy.

"Or otherwise," said Cathy, latching onto the logic, "what would Mary be doing out late at night riding around with Pike Early and two strangers?"

"And drinking hard," said Roy.

"Not what you'd expect from a middle school math teacher," said Cathy.

"Well, people can surprise you," said Roy philosophically.

"Yeah, and it looks like trouble's really come home to roost for Lori and her dad now."

"Yeah," said Roy. "That's the thing. You get used to setting a certain number of plates at the table…"

"And now they're down to two," said Cathy.

They both took long, breathy sips of their coffee. Then Roy put his cup down with a sharp, solid sound that was normal—and therefore comfortable—for their kitchen.

"Six for us, though. Right?" said Roy.

"That's right," she said reassuringly. "Six for us."

Again, they both took easy sips of coffee as they absorbed the power of their shared clarity. Yet Roy needed something more, and he pressed on cautiously.

"Why are you here, Cath?"

"I heard the coffee," she said with mild amusement.

"No, I mean, why are you with me?"

"Ohhh, well, you and I both know the answer to that one."

"Tell me anyway," he said as he wrinkled his nose to lift his glasses back into their proper position.

"Okay. Well, it's all because of something my grandma once told me. That if I should ever find myself a truly good man, I'd do well to never let him go. Because there just aren't that many."

Roy looked up and past Cathy. He fixed his eyes on the daybreak view out their kitchen window, shook his head ever so slightly, and exhausted a small, sarcastic chuckle of disbelief.

"Yeah, well, I gotta say. That still sounds pretty lame to me," he said.

"*Your* problem," replied Cathy. "Not mine."

A Night by the Fire

George Howard lives life with an uncertain sense of direction. Nobody is more aware of this fact than George himself. It's not something he's especially proud of, but neither is it a source of self-loathing. At worst, George's tendency to get turned around earns him the odd verbal jab of the most playful sort, typically delivered with a wink and a wicked grin by his best friend and regular hunting companion, Ivan Thrower.

"Hell, George. If you didn't get yourself a little by-God lost every now and then, huntin' with the likes of you would be a mighty poor excuse for entertainment," Ivan was fond of saying. "And then what would I do?"

George is never the target of true scorn, because he's the sort of guy most people like.

Walking across the open country with his rifle low to his side and balanced in one hand, George is a striking figure—tall, trim, square-shouldered, with just enough meat on his bones to see him through several days without food. George is inadvertently muscular, which his new wife attributes to a mix of his hard work and his lineage: a Catholic farm family of wise-acre boys and gritty girls, from which she snagged him with the promise of a different kind of life. He walks the countryside with a long stride and an easy pace, which is just slow enough to make Ivan crazy, leading them to split up on hunts, following roughly parallel paths with only occasional sightings of one another.

Even from the vertical distance that now separates them on the upper flanks of Tumblejack Mountain, Ivan can make out his friend's likeable face. George's cheeks become well-defined when he smiles, the upper parts taking on a roundness that complements the pronounced angle of his jaw, and the smile lines that radiate out from the corners of his small but welcoming eyes. Ivan can see all of this clearly, at first from his view well down the mountain, and then, as they move apart, in his mind.

Throughout his life, George has gotten credit for being a person who smiles a lot. And he's never minded that. But he's always had to admit to himself that he's unworthy of the credit. It's all on account of his pale blue eyes, which are somewhat sensitive to light. When the sun presents itself with any sort of vigor, George squints. Which looks to the world like a great big smile. So even on days when his eyes are gray and his mood is as forbidding as a squall, George is seen as a smiler. Again, that's fine with him.

Hunting with Ivan is also fine with George. After all, Ivan pretty much taught George how to hunt in the first place.

§

That education began at the plywood mill. They barely knew each other at first, except to nod hello on their way to and from the grubby green lunchroom. George worked the spreaders, where he was one of many men applying the black liquid adhesive to layers of veneer that came together to become plywood. George had no idea where Ivan worked in the mill, but he knew his name all too well because Ivan had a reputation among the millworkers. He was known as lazy, a drinker, a womanizer, and a sometimes fighter. But more than anything else, Ivan was known to be whip-ass smart, and he was famous for talking faster than the average man can think.

One Friday toward the end of the shift, the day-foreman walked up and stood beside George, and the two of them spent a silent minute in the cacophony of the mill, watching two millwrights repair the notoriously unreliable spreader equipment. When the foreman finally spoke to George, it was without turning his gaze from the backsides of the millwrights.

"George, come next Monday morning, I guess the man upstairs wants you out on the pond saw."

"Temporary deal?"

"Nope."

"Balls!"

"Hell, George, I figured you'd like being out in the fresh air and all," said the foreman, who was mildly amused by the reaction.

"Naw, the fresh air's fine. But I don't know a good goddamn about runnin' that pond saw, and I'll prob'ly foul it up somehow."

"I just don't see that you've got a problem," said the smiling foreman. "'Cause the way I figure it, this whole damn mill has been fucked-up from the first day. Top to bottom. From that bright shiny office up there in the rafters to that row of one-hole crappers out back. It's a genuine clusterfuck all around. So you'd have to do something pretty damn stupid to even get noticed out there in the pond shack. Besides, they're teaming you with Ivan Thrower. And compared to him, you're an alter boy. Gotta piss, Georgy. See ya."

On Monday, George took his first unsteady steps down the bouncy catwalk that leads from the bank of the millpond to the floating shack—corrugated metal siding with rust here and there, poorly secured to the wooden framing inside. When George reached out to brace himself against the shack, the metal gave in to his weight, popping with a cannon-like roar that exploded out the opposite side of the three-walled lean-to. George had intended a quieter entrance.

"Jesus!" shouted a man's voice from inside. "Did the lightning hit anybody that matters?"

"Near as I can tell, it didn't hit me," offered George as he entered the pond shack uncomfortably. "But I guess that doesn't really answer your question, seein' as how you don't know me yet."

"Well, I'll be damned. They sent me another one," said Ivan, who was seated in a feeble wooden chair next to a roaring woodstove that the millwrights had welded up out of an old oil drum.

"Another what?"

"Why, another man who's yet to put on his first pair of corks. And my god, let me inspect those boots of yours. Brand new?

"Yeah."

"From Jenkins'?"

"Yeah, and they cost me about as much as my first automobile."

"Oh, these are pretty. But let me ask you something—"

"It's George."

"And my name's Ivan, by the way. But what I want to know, George, is two things: One, have you ever been anywhere near a millpond before? And two, do you hunt? Because if the answer to both is no, well, I can teach you both. Now according to the flatulent fool who signs our paychecks up there in the office, it's my job to teach you what you need to know to get along out here. And I'll do it, by God. Even though I get damned tired of repeating myself to every new pair of boots they shuffle in my direction. And don't you believe he doesn't know I get tired of repeating myself, because that insipid sonofabitch doesn't really care for me. And I don't care for him. And he knows it. And that's just fine with Ivan, by God."

"Yeah?"

"Yeah, I'll teach you well, George. So good, in fact, that if I ever turn up dead, that sonofabitch can turn my job right over to you, and this miserable mill won't spend a candy-ass second waiting on logs to come up from the pond. And it won't be because of anything that embarrassment of a boss ever did. No, it'll be because I taught you how to do the job better than that imperial prick ever imagined it could be done. And he'll know it was me. He'll know I won. And that's enough to make me smile even if I'm face down in the muck at the bottom of this God-forsaken pond."

"Sounds like a sad state of affairs for you," said George. "'Cause I ain't never been on the pond before. And the only deer I ever killed is the one I bounced offa my Merc."

Ivan adjusted himself in the creaky old chair, sliding back in order to bend at the waist to finish lacing up his tired-looking corks. On the makeshift table next to him sat a battered steel thermos that looked every bit as grimy as George's new surroundings. And next to that, a green coffee cup that had been filled and emptied countless times but washed only rarely. Looking up at George from his boot-lacing posture, Ivan's eyes were strangely intense. The nearly black irises were in strong contrast to the whites of his eyes, which seemed unduly clear for a man of his reputation. His forehead wrinkled up in uniform folds of thin, tanned flesh. His shiny black hair went straight back and low to the scalp, giving Ivan a look of constant severity.

"You look like a two-eighty man to me," said Ivan.

"How's that?"

"The .280 Remington, George. A pump action deer rifle favored by Zane Grey. You seem like the kind of guy who ought to own one. It isn't glamorous or anything, but it's got pretty good knock-down power."

"You know Zane Grey?"

"Hell no. But I've read just about every book he's written. And I've read plenty about him. You care much for Mr. Grey?"

"Some."

"Is that right?," said Ivan Thrower, who seemed pleased.

§

Owing to years of working and hunting together, George and Ivan are known as a prolific and successful hunting team. They hardly ever come home empty-handed. Some years, they take enough deer to feed several families; something of a violation in the eyes of the game warden, who nobody likes. But the two of them know better than to brag about their hunting accomplishments, which could cost them many times the price of the Remington .280 that George, on Ivan's advice, had long since adopted as his signature firearm.

That they dress somewhat alike has become part of the local color. Not that George and Ivan ever set out to look like twins. It's just that practicality wins out over vanity. For one thing, it rains during the Oregon hunting season as much as it doesn't. Which means they've got to have some way to stay dry. So both wear plastic rain hats, even when it's not raining. They are fairly broad-rimmed like small cowboy hats. George and Ivan got the only two colors available from the manufacturer. Ivan's is red. George's is gray. Both wear an accompanying leather shoelace that feeds down through little holes just above the ears, hanging loosely below the chin and knotted to keep the wooden cinch bead from falling off. When it rains, George and Ivan wear their hats low on their foreheads, just above the eyebrows. When the sun shines, they tilt their hats all the way up, revealing the entirety of their faces, making them look a little like young cowpokes on their first visit to a saloon. But no one ever comments openly on how George and Ivan look. Because for the most part, people are intimidated by Ivan and respectful of George.

In preparation for a hunt, George and Ivan make a ritual out of greasing the brown leather uppers of their hunting boots, to make them waterproof. They sit by the cast iron woodstove in Ivan's unimpressive house, drinking black coffee and talking and smoking cigarettes that they roll themselves. It's a leisurely but important process that centers on warming the boots and a can of grease by the fire, and then brushing on layer after layer of the grease, which has been liquefied by the heat. The combination of heavy, unfiltered smoke, and pungent boot grease creates an aroma that somehow makes the conversation seem more important, more meaningful, more vital. But it's also enough to drive Ivan's current girlfriend, whoever she might be, first to the opposite end of the shotgun-style house, and then unceremoniously out of the house, which suits them just fine. Because inevitably, the conversation turns to the hunt at hand. And at that point, distractions are unwelcome.

Planning their Tumblejack hunt prompts George and Ivan to be even more animated than usual as they slather grease and slurp coffee. Because unlike their typical hunt, which has them pushing through the same brushy forests along the same familiar game trails, this hunt is to be far from the comfort and familiarity of the river canyon they call home.

True, Ivan has hunted Tumblejack Mountain once, years before. But he was young and mostly drunk, so all he really remembers is that the Mule Deer there are monstrous. Which is all the motivation necessary for Ivan to talk George into making the five-hour drive to Tumblejack country.

Sitting in straight-back chairs, their laceless boots glistening with grease, George and Ivan study a very old Forest Service map of Tumblejack. It is so worn that its creases were fuzzy with wood pulp fragments, and major sections are completely missing. In fact, the spot Ivan figured to pitch camp is obscured by an ancient fold that has long since given up any attempt to show roads and creeks and elevation lines. But this is not a problem. Because the friends are much more concerned about other issues. For example, what kind of food should they take? How exactly do you get to Tumblejack? Whose car is best for the drive? Where might they stop along the way for a meal? Would there be a liquor store available somewhere between home and the hunt? These are the issues that carry weight.

Ivan's '54 Ford Club Wagon is deemed most suitable for the drive. It is also decided that they'd take a good supply of bacon and eggs and pancake flour for breakfast, and venison jerky for the field. As for evening meals, they take a more cavalier approach. The plan is to take frozen Navy bean soup for the first night, and a sack of potatoes and a big iron skillet for the remaining nights. The idea being that there would be camp meat to cook, which requires that someone shoot something edible very early on in their visit to Tumblejack.

§

It is only during the long drive that Ivan reveals precisely how little he remembers about the lay of the land on Tumblejack. It isn't so much that he had lied to George. But Ivan has a way of not letting people get too concerned about the degree of his honesty or accuracy when telling stories. Especially his hunting stories. Because Ivan learned as a very young man growing up in the Texas Hill Country that if a person works enough random detail into a tale, people tend to buy it. It was a lesson taught to him by a unexcitable cowboy named Jim, who had a horse named Hot Helen, and who could sit on the porch for hours on humid summer evenings, telling stories while fireflies traced lines in the heavy Texas air. Ivan thrived on those firefly stories.

George isn't exactly shocked to hear an updated version of Ivan's account. In fact, George kind of enjoys his friend's habit of trickling out the truth. He has a genuine patience for the game that few people could muster. Which has everything to do with why these two are friends at all.

Within a few months of being paired up on the pond, they are each other's best friend in life. This friendship becomes fodder for lunchroom talk at the mill. People are confounded as to why nice, reasonable George would put up with the endless hazing and horseplay and clever half-truths of a joker like Ivan.

Hunting with Ivan has its risks. That's what flits through George's mind upon learning that Ivan is substantially less sure of things than previously indicated. But there they are, the club wagon packed to its fuzzy cloth ceiling with clothes and guns and greasy boots and sleeping bags and food and lanterns and a Coleman stove and some pitch-laden firewood and an Army surplus wall tent that is big enough for a staff meeting, cruising toward Tumblejack. And even though apprehension keeps repeating itself like reflector posts on the shoulder of the road, George is glad to be going. Because his disgust with living fearfully is more powerful than his fear of getting lost.

A confident three-point blacktail buck walks slowly across the two-lane mountain highway, casually aware of the silent blue object hurdling toward it on the long, steep upgrade. It steps from the coarse, porous pavement onto the crunchy red cinders of the shoulder, stops, and turns its head to see two broad smiles through the windshield as the Ford roars by.

"Jesus God Almighty, Georgy! Did ya see that big sonof abitch?"

"Well, seein' as how you nearly turned him into a hood ornament, I got a pretty good look."

I'm tellin' ya, Georgy. Where we're goin', they'd arrest a man for takin' somethin' that puny."

George says nothing in response, because his mind has already wandered off, just as the three-point has done.

A few miles farther down the road, George and Ivan come upon a sight even more compelling than the buck they'd seen. A car on the side of the road. Two women. One flat tire. And for Ivan, a situation that he simply cannot drive past.

They are unarresting women. But in Ivan's eyes, in this remote setting on a mountain highway with little or no traffic, these women deserve every bit of charm and energy Ivan has at his disposal. George is shy with women. Rather than stand awkwardly in witness to Ivan's social skills, he picks up the tire iron and proceeds to finish the job the women had begun. With a noisy audience of three at his back, George quietly does the work, accenting the conversation only with the occasional tinny clink of a lug nut landing in the upside-down hub cap. George has the tire changed and the flat in the trunk long before the flirtatious conversation reaches its full potential. George is relieved to end the encounter, even though he enjoys watching Ivan work. George always makes allowances for Ivan when it comes to women, because he knows Ivan's story. His history. He knows why Ivan is the way he is. And where women are concerned, he knows that Ivan always has some catching up to do: Ivan had been betrayed by his first and only wife while he was off in the Pacific, fighting the good fight, unaware of what awaited him back home.

§

The main road leading into Tumblejack country from the highway is a fine gravel creation. It was mostly straight and flat, and it is maintained by a road crew that takes obvious pride in its work. George and Ivan judged it to be a road worth taking. And even the billowing dust isn't all that bad, because it justifies their inclination to sip cold beer from stubby brown bottles. With George now behind the wheel, the heavy Ford plows down two of the three available tracks. The flathead V-8 hums in a coarse but pleasing harmony with the wind rush of open wing windows, and with the crunchy roar of fat tires smothering gravel, all of which is accented by a random percussion of crushed rock striking the underside of the wagon. It is a soothing sound to the men whose feet feel the impact of bigger rocks in the floorboard. It is reassuring, too, because both men had grown up hearing pieces of gravel pinging off the suspensions of their dads' vehicles. Both men grew up knowing the distinct, solid sound of a rock striking the exhaust manifold, and the disturbing sound of a tall rock making contact with the oil pan. It's not something they ever talk about, or even think about in a fully conscious way. But the sound of backroad gravel on Detroit metal serves as a crude kind of score. A kind of traveling music for people on the road to somewhere. In this case, it is theme music for an unfamiliar hunt, the thought of which fires their desire to get there.

§

Milepost 139. It is the only indication of the road they seek.

"Go about a half mile past the marker," counsels Ivan. "And take 'er easy, or you'll be past it before you see it."

George slows the hulking Ford just in time to discover the narrow entrance to Stone Corral Road, which has no right to be called a road at all. It is a dirt track decorated with boulders and disfigured by runoff water surging down the mountainside during summer thundershowers. George takes his time, dodging the most threatening obstacles, weaving his way up the draw that was one of many draws on the east side of Tumblejack Mountain.

"Funny damn looking mountain," says George as he pulls the wagon onto a kind of natural landing that would become their camp. "There ain't hardly a tree to be seen."

"Hell, man. We've got junipers all around. Don't they count?"

"Tall bushes."

"Well now I'll tell you what," says an instantly defensive Ivan, his black eyes reduced to slits of rebuttal. "We got all the damned trees we'll ever need back home in the canyon, and sometimes I get sicka lookin' at 'em. Because they're big and they're tall, and they make the sky seem small, and I just don't think that's very friendly. So by my way of thinking, this wide open country is a pretty nice change. It feels right. And if you're gonna get all disagreeable about things," lightening his tone with a flickering grin, "I'll have no choice but to knock a turd out of you a foot long. Maybe that'll improve the view."

"I reckon we'd better get that tent put up, seein' as how someone needs a nap."

"Nap, hell! I need a snort."

That there is a level spot at all is significant. There is just enough room for the Ford, the wall tent, a makeshift lean-to for cooking and eating, and a fire pit. The division of labor had not been previously discussed. But after a few years of doing this sort of thing, both George and Ivan know how things go.

Fire comes first. George sets out to find the appropriate rocks to make the fire ring. Meanwhile, Ivan lights up a handmade cigarette and wanders in big looping circles around the edges of the flat in search of twigs and small limbs and other debris that might serve as kindling. The modest armful of stuff Ivan returns with is pitiful—he drops it beside the imposing fire ring George built.

As the two stop momentarily to consider their progress, the air begins to move past them. It is as if the air encasing them there on the side of Tumblejack Mountain exists as a solid unit. A single mass. And when it begins to move, that mass slabs off, like a great wall of blue-white Alaska glacier calving off into a bitter, icy bay.

The movement of air changes things.

The dust that had been hanging in the air since they rolled up the dirt track is instantly gone. The warm, pungent smell of the junipers is replaced by a crisper, cleaner, more vital scent. The near-silence of a warm October afternoon is now usurped by the overwhelming but gentle sound of wind brushing across an entire mountainside, slipping through the junipers at every level, making the mountain seem to breathe. It moves through the tall brown grasses. It moves through the low scrub brush. It curls around the craggy edges of basalt outcroppings. It touches everything. It cools everything. It serves notice to everything. Every creature.

The change is not lost on the hunters, who unconsciously return to the task of pitching camp. George takes the lead. With a minimum of wasted motion, and with a sharp eye for knowing exactly where to position things for maximum efficiency and ease of use, George crafts their camp in the unspoken name of common sense. The ax goes to a place about five paces from the fire ring, on the upwind side. The Coleman lantern goes to a hook that is just below the junction of three slender poles that had been lashed to the top of the Club Wagon, and are now lashed together again to form a crooked but reliable tripod, configured to let lantern light spread evenly over the camp from a height of about five feet. The lean-to is constructed from members of the same family of crooked poles as a framework for a threadbare canvas tarp: a back wall and a slanted roof.

Ivan respects George's talent for this work. And though he is not exactly helpless himself, he'd long ago learned to recognize those times when it's best to stay out of George's way. Ivan is particularly amused by one of George's greatest efficiencies, which is the use of old inner tubes. His method is to cut the black, pungent rubber into long, thin strips that can bind just about anything together. This includes long, skinny poles that don't look strong enough to support their own weight. George figures there isn't anything that can't be brought under control and put to work with the proper application of inner tubes. It's just a matter of using your head and thinking things through. George had proven to Ivan that whatever the task, whatever the challenge at hand, it can be overcome with a little time and a few strips of black magic.

The camp comes together. All the gear is in its place, and the fire is fully alive. Situated on the eastern side of Tumblejack, they had been in the shadows since the moment of arrival. Now, their entire view of the world is retreating toward darkness. And that is fine with both men. Because they know that except for cranking up the Coleman and cooking up a little something to eat, the hard part of the day is done. And in the morning, well before the sun returns, they will hunt.

Ivan cooks. Which is to say, he plops the mostly melted Navy bean soup into a dented, blackened pot with an uneven bottom, and then chases the beans and hunks of ham in circles with a wooden spoon. The unsteady pot shifts on the Coleman's wire rack, producing a repetitive metal-on-metal noise that is amplified by the green metal body of the stove. Encouraged by the blue flame of white gas, the soup soon becomes a feast. It is thick and heavily flavored by the ham and salt. The beans are a click shy of firm, which gives them a good, satisfying bite and a pleasing consistency. It is soup that requires chewing. And when the saltiness builds up, Ivan is ready with the cure.

"How's about a snort?" he says to George with his trouble-maker grin.

Seagram's 7 and a swig of water is Ivan's solution for most situations. In this instance, George allows to himself that Ivan is on the money. Because salt is no match for whiskey.

By the time George and Ivan tip their bowls up to get the last reluctant morsels, the night is lit only by stars, their campfire, and their Coleman lantern. There is no moon. Which is good, because it means the deer will stay bedded down for the night, waiting for first light to begin foraging. That's when George and Ivan plan to meet them in the field.

But that particular pleasure is hours away. And since neither man relishes the first night's sleep, almost always a restless one, they opt to stay by the fire and have more Seagram's 7 for dessert. Finally, when their energy for conversation plays out, they sack out.

No alarm clock is necessary to wake them. They sleep as poorly as anticipated, feeling every pebble and hearing every sound. So getting up is a distinct relief. Plus, there is an urgency. The kind that always kicks in when hunters start wondering whether they remembered everything they meant to bring. And whether they brought the proper socks. And whether to start out wearing two layers of shirts or three in the cold pre-dawn air, remembering that things warm up quickly once they start moving.

Everything metal is cold and unfriendly to the touch. Everything cloth is only slightly less chilled. The sky is black and still, showcasing the heavens in a way that almost makes George feel religious and insignificant. Daybreak approaches slowly. With each glance eastward, the horizon is incrementally lighter. George and Ivan leave camp with coffee in their bellies, jerky in their pockets, and ammunition on their belts.

§

The dirt road follows a draw that had been created by countless centuries of runoff from summer gully washers and spring melts. But the route is dry and noisy in the predawn, and impossible to see. They move as slowly as the approaching sunrise, making sure of each footfall, as if walking by Braille, trying not to trip or turn an ankle. By the time their lungs are chugging to capacity up the forbidding road, they begin to see gray shapes, which soon reveal themselves to be rocks. In front and high above them, they can make out the western horizon, which is the basalt architecture of Tumblejack.

The uncertainty of the dark walk is replaced by the realization that if they can see horizon lines of any sort, they can also see the silhouette of antlers against a dim sky. And with that, the hunt is on. Without saying a word—not that they could, given their shared history with cigarette smoke—both men pump cartridges into their respective chambers, and both men feel rewarded by the familiar dull tinkling sound of brass being muted by the gunpowder it contains.

By the time George and Ivan crest the shoulder of the unforested mountain, their eyes are no longer dilated for darkness. The stars are gone. The sky behind them reinvents itself as the full spectrum of sunlight grips the distant eastern mountains, emerging one color at a time, changing from nearly black to dark purple to dull gray to pale orange to bright red to whatever the day may bring.

A huge piece of the earth is suddenly the sole property of these two hunters—with dry grass, gnarly junipers, rocky outcroppings, and distant rimrocks decorated with golden aspen groves at their base. And well above the rimrocks, the true top of Tumblejack, which is high enough to have its own little cloud formation hovering near its rounded peak. The mountaintop seems aloof and arrogant, and fully prepared to dispute land rights with the trespassers.

"Damn," says George.

"Isn't that something?"

"Damn it to hell, Ivan. This is bigass country."

"It's only big because you haven't walked it yet."

"Come again?"

"C'mon. You know how it is, Georgy. Getting from here to there only looks impossible 'til you do it. After that, you own the bastard."

"I reckon we oughta keep it down out here," which is George's way of saying it is time to quit talking and start hunting. Ivan obliges with a casual hand gesture that aims the hunters into the wind to begin a giant sweep toward the north side of Tumblejack; a maneuver that had been discussed the night before over Navy beans and Seagram's 7.

The first hunt takes up the whole of the morning, during which the two friends move in distant unison, tracing a meandering arc around the broad basin that cradles them. With the sun as squarely above them as it can be in October in Oregon, they stop to talk it over, each of them taking a perch on a basalt ledge, within easy earshot of each other's low voice. They report on the fresh sign they had seen. And the warm beds they'd stumbled across. Pulling hard on the salty venison jerky from George's homemade smoker, they agree that they are indeed in the right neighborhood, and that big brown eyes are probably watching them as they talk.

The meeting on the rocks signals the conclusion of the *planned* portion of their long hunting weekend. They had already covered the little piece of Tumblejack Ivan actually knows. To make things more interesting, their Forest Service map is back in camp, right next to the cold coffee pot, right where Ivan had left it.

"Time to shoot from the seat of our pants," says Ivan, seizing the opportunity to trot out his favorite self-deprecating cliché.

"That sounds about right," replies an unimpressed but amused George.

From where they sit, getting back to camp and the unattended map would have been easy. But there are valuable hours of proper daylight remaining, and the men are exhilarated by the pureness of the air and the moment, and they are somewhat numb with opening day ambition. They hatch a mapless plan to hunt fully around the highest parts of the mountain that looks down on them. They decide to leave their now-familiar basin on the east side of Tumblejack, to exit it as high as they can up the flank of the peak, and to begin side-hilling their way around the top until such time as they return to the opposite side of the basin.

Recalling the tattered map in his head, Ivan observes that their second hunt will take them places the map couldn't have shown them anyway, because that part of the map is tattered.

Still, George is willing, so long as they maintain a line of sight to each other.

"Agreed," says Ivan. "I'll even go low, so you can take your time."

This is an unusual kindness for Ivan-the-uncaring, because both men know all too well that when circling the flanks of a peak, the lower route is always longer. And often rougher, thanks to the likelihood of unforeseen ridges and ravines that must be crossed in the perpendicular.

They depart from the highest part of the basin together. But then George heads farther up the mountain, while Ivan heads somewhat down. As the distance between them grows, so does George's apprehension. He keeps glancing downward, finally prompting Ivan to flip George the finger; a crude display of affection that makes George grin.

Ivan drops down into his first ravine, and is gone from sight.

"Damn it," says George to the situation. "Don't it just figure."

§

Now a man alone, George embarks on what becomes an hours-long march around a mountaintop that is, much to George's regret, larger and more complex than he expects. He is preoccupied with three simple goals: Keeping an eye out for Ivan, not turning an ankle as he picks his way across steep slopes with rolling rocks, and eventually making it back to camp. Absorbed by these pursuits, George is slow to realize two other key elements of opening day on Tumblejack.

First, he is no longer hunting. And second, the sun that warmed him and Ivan at mid-day is replaced by a high, gray, seamless ceiling that has neither detail nor dimension. The air has cooled, as have the tip of his nose and the lobes of his ears.

Time is now as homogenous as the sky. Lacking a watch or a sun to tell him what hour it is, George continues his slow scramble around Tumblejack's rocky crown, hoping for a glimpse of Ivan. But what he sees instead is a humorless sky lowering its disapproving brow. Soon, it comes to George that it is probably time to make for camp however he can. He breaks from his self-imposed route and drops down the mountain several yards in a focused effort to spot his friend, expecting to find Ivan lagging behind his own progress around Tumblejack, hoping they can simply head for camp together. But that's when George stumbles onto the craggiest truth of the day…

He finds himself standing at the lip of nothingness. Absent-mindedly lowering the butt of his rifle to the ground in resignation, George speaks to the unexpected scene.

"I'll be go to Hell."

It is as if the west side of Tumblejack is missing. Every bit as missing as the section of map that would have portrayed this terrain. There is no slope to match the side they'd approached from. No alpine grass. No scrubby junipers. No alluring Aspen groves. Nothing.

Instead, George sees a rocky abyss. A great, empty amphitheater with an audience of one, which up to that point has been blocked from George's view by the higher parts of the mountain, tucked away just below his horizon line. It is as if the god of lost hunters has taken an unearthly scoop and carved out a massive serving of Tumblejack. And in the distance down the mountain, farther away than a reasonable hunter would try to shoot, is the opposite edge of this nothingness. That, George suddenly understands, is as far as Ivan got before aborting his assignment and reversing his course. George's mind races to comprehend what Ivan has long since realized; that this particular hunt should never have been attempted.

George never fears being alone. But on those rare occasions when he finds himself geographically alone, his inner voice gains a certain clarity. This is one of those times.

He is a hundred yards uphill from the precipice before realizing he's already begun his scramble to make camp before dark. He's already concluded that he's come too far to reverse course, and that a perilous hike straight up over the top of

Tumblejack now would be the height of foolishness. Indeed, common sense instructs George to continue on around as planned, on his original route. But to be damn quick about it.

"Go, man. Go," he encourages himself.

George becomes a blur to himself. He is aware only of the sound his boots make as they scruf against the rocks and dirt, and the sound his pant legs make as they carry him through low, brittle brush, and the sound his heart makes as it echoes up through his throat and open mouth. Eventually, he crests a ridge that promises to reveal exactly where George is in relation to camp. And it does.

But the truth of the view is both good and bad: the point at which he and Ivan had entered the basin that morning appears to be all of two miles away as the crow flies. But, George knows he cannot get there before the graying sky turns black.

"Better get farther down off of here," he says without speaking. "Better get down where there's a little shelter. Better get myself in a position to head out in the morning. Better prepare myself for a long night. Better hope my matches work."

As he drops down the mountain and into the basin, he is comforted to know pretty much where he is. Yet there is a disturbing double urgency in the air, because there is a race between the dark gray clouds and the darkness itself. A race to see which can reach George first. A race to discover which might be the first to hide the top of Tumblejack from George's wide open eyes. A race to stop George in his tracks, and to make him think about things.

This isn't at all like being lost, George rationalizes. But the weather and the darkness argue an opposing view.

§

The blackness comes all the way down to the ground. The terrain that previously surrounded George is gone. And as he stares at the small, struggling fire he built of twigs and sticks, he also struggles to remember how things had looked in the light of day. He struggles to understand how he had once again managed to get himself in a predicament, and how he would manage to explain this turn of events to the unforgiving Ivan Thrower, who has an eerily accurate sense of direction, even when thoroughly drunk. It is cold, which somehow makes the night just that much blacker, just that much closer in on him. Yet the fire is good, with enough brightness and motion to at least allow George the illusion that he is not completely alone. He no longer holds his rifle, because the only thing he can see to shoot is the fire itself. And that fire is his new best friend, and the object of his full attention. The air is still. The flames and smoke go straight up into the blackness, quickly disappearing from George's new small world. Striking a comfortable, military-style at-ease posture, George fixates on the flames. He senses no danger. Or risk. But he realizes that if his young wife knew of his immediate circumstance, she would worry. And the mere thought of this troubles George instantly, because she's fragile, with the kind of blue eyes that constantly ask for help. Her eyes are with him constantly. He sees them vividly. Just as he had when they first met on the back porch of the old farmhouse where they both happened to be visiting. It was the home of his brother-in-law's parents, who happened to be her aunt and uncle. George had been embarrassed because he'd been working in the barn without a shirt. She had been perched on the porch bench, wearing a white blouse and a long skirt that announced her Barbara Stanwick waist. The sight of her had undone him. The sparks between them had posed a fire danger to the nearby hay fields that laid in windrows, drying in the sun. And from that moment to this, George has been a constant captive of her desperately blue eyes.

The largest stick on George's fire falls into the coals, abruptly commanding his attention. More fuel is in order. George breaks his stance and moves to the perimeter of his fire's light for more debris to burn. The ground is fairly littered with the dead remains of woody plants, most of which are crunchy to walk on and quite dry. Some of the bigger sticks snap under his boots, sounding for the world like blackcaps on the Fourth of July. Wandering on the edge of darkness and collecting firewood with a complete lack of urgency, George remembers how he and his two closest brothers used to torment summertime bats with firecrackers. The idea was to secure a firecracker to a decent-sized rock, usually with thin strips of old innertube, and then cradle that rock and firecracker in the leather pouch of a slingshot, which one of the rascally brothers had pulled back into firing position. Then another brother would strike a wooden match and light the fuse, which was the cue to hurdle that rock and firecracker into the dark blue evening sky over the barnyard, which was where the farm's family of bats preferred to dine on flying insects, diving this way and that in quick pursuit of supper. To the bats, an airborne rock read like a feast on sonar, meaning they always gave hot chase, first on the upward trajectory, and then on the unavoidable fall to earth. The chase was fun to watch even without firecrackers. But it was the highest form of fun to watch those bats react to mid-air explosions. Half the time, the boys would end up on the ground, laughing uncontrollably at the misfortune of the bats, which George had always detested since being frightened by a bat in broad daylight, which meant it was probably rabid.

George's fire leans off center now. A barely-there breeze comes from behind George, and the change in the flame brings him back to Tumblejack. He glances to his wrist, where a watch ought to be, and supposes that he's already been standing by the fire for hours. He does not expect Ivan to come looking for him, because as they discussed many times, the smartest thing you can do if you get stuck or lost is to hold your position until the return of daylight. Take shelter if the weather says so. And if at all possible, build yourself a damn good fire. Flames, smoke, motion and warmth. It occurrs to George how roundly reassuring these things can be. Like the time when he was ten or so, and he got caught miles from home in a big summer rain.

There he was in t-shirt and overalls, walking down the long gravel road that led to his own gravel driveway, getting soaked. From behind him came a dark green International pick-up, which slowed to a crawl as it got beside him. The passenger door opened to reveal a lean-looking farmer with a weekend's worth of beard and a cigarette in his mouth. A ride was kindly offered and eagerly accepted. Inside the old pick-up, it was dry. And comfortable. Even though the atmosphere of the cab was blue with rich, fresh smoke. It smelled good to George. Thick. Earthy yet unearthly. Protective, somehow. The driver didn't talk so much as he grunted and gestured. So George also kept quiet, choosing instead to study the hard metal dashboard, with its satin green paint and its chrome knobs for the choke and the radio and the windshield wipers, which managed to keep just ahead of the rain, enabling the farmer and George to see the dark gravel road ahead, and eventually the galvanized steel mailbox that marked the end of George's driveway. The farmer behind the wheel knew to stop, and did, and then waved his glowing cigarette to suggest George should exit the smoky comfort of the cab. His lungs felt the first cold shot of clean air, and he instantly missed the warmth of the farmer's smoke.

The wind moves again, and is no longer at George's back. But the small fire pays little attention. George takes the few steps necessary to get near his rifle, which is resting on a piece of juniper burl, with its butt in the dirt and its muzzle in the air. George bends over to feel the action, which is very cold. This bothers George a little. Because to him, a warm action has always been a sign of recent activity and attention. And a cold action always connotes a complete lack of action, an unpleasant brand of nothingness, which to George is a form of sadness. He decides to hold his rifle for a while, balancing it in his right hand, with the action at the axis point, his arm fully extended toward the ground, steady with an affected sense of purpose. "That's better," he says to the fire. Aware of his own army-like posture, George begins to miss his older brother, Bud, whose given name was Lowell, and who had been an Army corporal when he drove a Jeep off the ramp of a Higgins boat on Omaha Beach. George had heard the story many times. But no matter how often he replayed it in his head, George could not fully comprehend how his brother had managed it all. How Bud had the wherewithal to drive the Jeep directly into the maelstrom of fire from the German 88s, which had the complete advantage as they fired mercilessly, endlessly from their elevated bunkers at the top of the beach. How Bud popped the clutch to launch the Jeep down the ramp, its windshield locked down and out of the way so as not to be shattered. How, upon finding the end of the ramp, Bud's Jeep became completely submerged in the red Omaha surf. How the Jeep ran anyway, owing to the fact that Bud had completely slathered the engine in a heavy layer of waterproofing grease, and to the fact that the air intake on the carburetor had been coupled to a tall pipe that went straight up into the air, allowing the Jeep to breath under water as it clawed the liquid sand with all four wheels in a frantic race for land and chaos. How Bud had to hold his breath as the Jeep breathed freely, hoping but not expecting to avoid getting hit by the 88s once that stubborn Jeep had found its footing in the red running sand, insanely digging and lurching, pulling itself over bodies of fallen men, as if it knew its mission better than did Bud. George never was able to understand how Bud lived through it, but he's always understood what a miracle it was to see Bud kick open the short, white frontyard gate on the day he came home from Europe, ready to carry on, with the Weeping Willows swirling around his head and shoulders, embracing him, in a warm afternoon breeze that carried the sweet scent of July hay in the barn. That beguiling aroma permeated the old farmhouse, reaching and filling every neglected corner of every room, including Bud's. That's where he unpacked his duffel with a measure of ceremony, putting his odd-feeling civilian clothes away in the long-empty closet, and then marching out back to the burn barrel, where he doused the duffel and his uniforms with diesel and lit them afire, glad to see them go. For the next

19 years, Bud stayed in that room, which was just above that of his aging parents. He made a living as a cat skinner and a welder, and later designed a corntopper that won the admiration of area corn growers who were eager to hire Bud to top their noisy green cornfields in August. George grew up admiring his older brother, because Bud worked hard and discovered smart ways to overcome obstacles. George also admired Bud's discretion, as evidenced by the fact that he'd fallen in love with the woman from the post office but kept it a complete secret from the family, save for George, who'd noticed that on days when Bud got mail, the large metal mailbox at the end of the driveway smelled faintly of dusty lilac perfume. George envied how Bud, at the conclusion of big family meals, would always manage to secure the first corner piece of the flat cake their mother made fresh each day. It was the most prized piece. And it came to be known as Bud's Corner. To George's way of thinking, it made considerable sense that he should take a corner piece of cake to his brother's grave every now and then. Although the first time George served dessert in the cemetery, complete with a fork and little blue plate that clinked loudly on the granite, he worried that someone might see his sentimentality. It's been a year since cancer took Bud. And on three quiet occasions, George has taken corner pieces of cake. But out of respect for his now dead brother's sense of discretion, he's told no one. Not even the fire, at which George continues to stare.

He studies it, carefully observing that it is very much like a small, glowing lodge. One with several small openings to the outside world, through which flows the fresh-chilled air of the night. The outside of the fire lodge is black and oddly shaped. Through the openings, though, George sees another realm. The threshold is grand, with sectioned embers glowing and then darkening with each wave of cool air being pulled inside the fire, like an old neon sign that blinks with an uncertain rhythm, unpredictable but inviting. Deep beyond the entrance, George sees a tantalizing wall of orange; large coals that glow with radiant clarity of purpose and a dedication of energy that makes human pursuits seem completely unimportant. Silly. Ridiculous, even. Drawn to the mysticism of fire and the painfully unattainable premise that anyone or anything might actually divine a purpose on earth, George goes inside. He becomes small . He does not burn, because George is a guest in a temple. A fiery grotto, where all the surfaces offer him visions of possibility and intrigue. Where every corner turned reveals a masterpiece. Where every passage explored has a reward. This place is happiness and hope. This place speaks not of the potential for goodness, but of the absolute prospect of it. The unblinking certainty of it. The died and gone to heaven truth of it. George is inside the fire. And he begins to fear his having to leave this wonderful spot. This incredible sensation. He wrestles with the realization that he cannot fully comprehend all that he witnesses here. That his mind and his sensibility are simply not up to the task of understanding and interpreting the truth and beauty of life as a fire.

George becomes even smaller. George is humbled. Yet he feels worthy. And while the only thing he fully understands is that he'll never really understand, he feels everything. And more than anything else, he feels love. Like a child exploring a cave, George wonders who had been here, inside the fire, before him. He searches the walls and the ceiling and floor for clues of previous visitors. But there is nothing. Because fire has no past, and no ability to reveal the history of others. There is only combustion in the present tense, and that is what gives fire its unabiding honesty. It burns away the unnecessary. It devours the disingenuous. It despises those who look away, avoiding their own truth. It is a friend to the willing, to those with quiet, internal courage. It is an enemy to all others. And while fire can certainly warm anyone who comes near, it can just as easily turn a chilled shoulder to those who, for whatever reason, lack the wherewithal to see beyond themselves. George is well beyond himself. And as he stands straight by the fire in the blackness of a Tumblejack night, he does not feel alone. Nor can he remember feeling any happier than he does at that moment. Fuel and oxygen are the ingredients of fire, but the unexpected by-product is a kind of contentment that survives the life and death of fire. This can never be taken away. And understanding only this, George grins into the fire, enchanted. Little wonder, then, that George does not immediately notice the tiny airborne ashes that come down around him. Miniscule flecks of whiteness, moving without benefit of wind. Delicately adrift, the ashes float in the calm air that has engulfs George and his friend the fire, quietly respectful of the silent dialogue between them and yet determined to make their entrance into George's consciousness.

Looking up from the fire and instantly realizing that his cheekbones are wet and his throat is tight with emotion, George also notices the new arrivals. But these are not ashes. This is snow. How odd it is to suddenly be surrounded by falling snow, George thinks to himself. How odd to have been wandering through an all-too-real catacomb of fire and mystery, only to exit amid the surreal qualities of falling snow. Small, dry flakes. Falling as slowly as the passage of time on a night when sleep keeps its distance. Falling but never failing, even after taking an eternity to make its way, to find a perfect landing place. Silently. Deliberately. Excruciatingly wonderful in its deportment. Like a tall dessert in an exquisite restaurant, snow has the pleasing element of surprise and wonder. A delight to even the harshest, least appreciative people. Snow is the moment of magic. Inexplicable in its ability to loosen the grip of dark moods and troubled lives. Inexhaustible in its propensity for making beleaguered adults feel like wide-eyed children. Intoxicating in its purest forms. Insightful in its gift for helping people see things, understand things, even as their view of the world around them becomes less and less defined. Perhaps it is the very vagueness of snow that causes people to know things they could not know before the arrival of snow. Perhaps. To George, though, snow is love. Now, at the age of thirty-four, the sight of falling snow never fails to overwhelm George with a kind of all-consuming joy. A fact that he's never shared with Ivan, for fear of retribution. But it's a fact of George's life. And since he is not a poet, he celebrates it without words.

Walking in falling snow one Saturday afternoon in the first winter weather of 1950, George found out about love. He was unprepared for it, though. It was unexpected. Because he'd only gone there, to her parents' house, because the arrival of snow earlier that day put him in a sociable mood. And because she'd asked him to come. He'd only expected to visit with her, maybe at the kitchen table in their rounded breakfast nook, and have a cup of Hills Brothers, with her mother buzzing around them. But Ruthie proposed a walk in the snow. Ruthie's mother liked that George was there, having previously noted that her sad daughter seemed happiest when young George comes by. She watched approvingly out the bathroom window as George and Ruthie marched away from house and up the narrow lane that went straight back to the foothills that rise to form the south wall of the broad canyon they all called home. George and Ruthie became two dark objects moving in the white infinity of snow, no bigger to Ruthie's mother's eye than the fence posts that line the lane, and then they were out of sight. Alone in the snow, the couple talked. Alone together as they had never been before, all they could see was each other. All they could hear were laughs and giggles and gentle words. All that mattered was that they were there. Together there in the snow, they sensed perfection. And George was helpless in the face of Ruthie's unassuming beauty. She was thoroughly covered except for her oval face, but it was her eyes that destroyed George. Perfect brown eyes. Smiling. Sparkling. Signaling the all clear. Setting the record straight with George, saying that she had set aside her fears. That she was ready to let George in, and to begin telling him her secrets. Her truths. So they stood at the end of the snowy lane, facing each other and their new truth. The space between them was gone. The world around them was insignificant. With clouds of steam forming from their mouths, with cheeks and noses flushed by winter wind and fresh emotion, with the squeaks and squawks of boots compacting fresh snow and heavy wool coats nestling into one another, they kissed the kiss of all kisses. And it snowed on them. And as they walked back down the lane toward the house, glove in glove, George was in awe of how he felt. And how perfect the day was. And how much he appreciated the falling of snow. And how, for the first time in his unremarkable life, he sensed an essential vitality in himself that superseded all self-perceptions that came before that afternoon with Ruthie in the snow. George was not equipped for this. But the decision was not his. So he wore the snow on his shoulders; pure white epaulets signifying his place among those who know what love is. He remembers all this vividly. He thinks of it frequently, even without the benefit of falling snow, because it is his version of hope. But this journey back to Ruthie had been especially strong.

As George's mind meanders back to the small fire on Tumblejack, he is slow to see that his situation is changing once again. Now the ground is more white than black, and the sky is noticeably less ominous, having brightened incrementally away from absolute darkness. *Snow changes everything for the better*, he thinks to himself. And in this instance, it is launching the process of changing night into day, thus relieving his fire of its responsibilities. George nudges the remaining coals with his boot, admiring the fire and saying this: *thanks for everything—good to have met you—maybe our paths will cross again—hope so.*

§

George is relieved at the prospect of continuing his much-delayed return to camp. The morning sky is much different than the one under which he and Ivan began their hunt. The sky and ground are dedicated to the exercise of sending and receiving snow, which now falls even more lightly. The clouds remain low, but no longer have the homogenous gray quality that says snow is imminent.

Rather, George can see all sorts of delicate shapes, which combine to create a silvery tunnel affect; a gossamer mobile that drags the ground with its misty sidewalls, but arches up just enough to reward George with yet another disarming view. It moves constantly, effortlessly, cinematically. It reminds him of an anniversary card he'd seen, all white and silver and unrealistically ornate, obscuring the grit and toil required to keep a marriage going for 25 years. This silvery tunnel lets a little of the painterly morning cloudlight reach the terrain below George, illuminating what he already recognizes as the way home. He heads downhill.

"Thanks," he says.

He finds his rhythm. His breathing and his footfalls are roughly syncopated. His pant legs brush against snow-encrusted ground cover, making more noise than a hunter should. But George is still not hunting. He is retreating. And he really doesn't care that if Ivan found out he was merely hiking back to camp on a morning that is God's gift to hunters, there'd be a price to pay. Ivan, who claims that he is never not a hunter, would sharpen his gaze in disapproval. He would question why a person would go to all the bother of preparing for a hunt, and then, when presented with nearly ideal conditions for tracking a big buck in virgin snow, opt not to hunt.

Should such a conversation occur, George would come up with something to satisfy Ivan's inquisition. But he would not tell the truth. He would not admit that hunting really isn't all that important to him. Nor would he try to articulate that what he stalks is not the animal. That what he craves is not the kill. George would circumvent all that, knowing that it might threaten the practiced rapport between them. Which is, in truth, what George values most. Because being with Ivan, having adventures with Ivan, introduces a vividness that would otherwise be lacking in his life.

§

George's legs suddenly break rhythm. They launch George upward, like a bobcat startled by a shotgun blast in the gravel beneath its paws. He stops breathing. His heart thunders. His brain races to interpret what he is hearing:

Air being ripped apart. Something being smacked smartly. The not too distant muzzle blast of what quickly identifies itself as a .270. The haunting echo of gunfire in the mountains, rolling through the snowy basin in search of an escape route to the sky, which happily devours the sound in its entirety, having built up its appetite after a busy night of silence.

Muscles tense and ears up, George quickly deciphers the situation: Ivan is up and hunting. Ivan had had a good night's sleep in a half-empty tent. He'd gotten himself up early, having sensed the snow. He'd made himself a short pot of cowboy coffee, and then sipped it down black as he warmed the action of his .270 in his other hand.

And now, George realizes, Ivan is out there with him. Hunting. Shooting. Taking a buck, which at that very moment is melting snow with its blood. George understands that he is very near the action, because the bullet passed close enough to be heard. That bullet struck in George's proximity with a superficial thwack that became a deep, meaty, muffled thud.

George comprehends that any moment, he and Ivan will greet one another. Playful words will be exchanged about his night out. George will fail in his attempt to explain that he spent a night alone on Tumblejack Mountain not because he'd gotten lost, but because he'd simply run out of time. He knows, too, that within a few minutes, he'll be field dressing Ivan's buck, because he'd long since gotten better at this unsavory task than the man who taught him. Then the two of them will sling their rifles over their shoulders, grab the antlers together with their free hands, and walk in unison as they drag Ivan's buck back to camp. Buddies on a hunt. Doing what they set out to do.

George knows, too, that they will break that camp in a couple of days. They'll stow it all in or on Ivan's Club Wagon, and then retrace the route of their drive to Tumblejack, which will seem much longer and slower than had the drive out. Upon arriving home, George will make the sounds he always makes when he steps onto his squeaky back porch, and then into his mudroom with its broken-down linoleum. He'll shed his coat and hat there, and then open the door into the part of his house that is heated by a woodstove. And there, George will greet his blue-eyed, small-waisted bride, who is troubled by these truths: that George values his friendship with Ivan Thrower over his marriage, that he's happiest after a hunt, and that he grows distant when it snows.

§

That thud George heard was a lie. It revealed just enough that cold morning on Tumblejack Mountain to let him draw the wrong conclusion, the way a winking storyteller spins a yarn, or a magician's sleight of hand fools an audience, or a philanderer comes up with yet another explanation to defuse his wife. That thud was a bullet. One that neither parted the hollow hair of a buck nor drew blood. One that didn't do what George thought at all.

The elasticity of time within the moment of stress allows George his imaginings, his speculations about what just happened and what might follow. Once stretched, though, time snaps back hard and takes George by the throat. It grabs him but good, shakes him, makes him see—understand—what that thud really was.

A miss.

Not ten feet behind where he stands in the sloping basin of Tumblejack, and rising up from the new snow like an altar, there also stands the rotting remains of a lone juniper tree. It grew where others refused to grow, but then died young to become a soft, decaying display of good intentions.

That dead tree, a gnarl of gray and dedicated to the loneliest of afterlives, received Ivan's projectile. George can see where the lead went in. He recognizes the damage done, because he had assassinated many a stump and snag himself.

But why? he wonders. *How?*

Ivan is not one to miss his target. His ability to aim and fire with calculable precision is more a matter of fact than legend, and few people in the North Santiam Canyon know of the truth of Ivan's marksmanship better than George. It is his goal to become the steely true shooter that Ivan is by nature. He is constantly going to school on Ivan, meaning the student knows his teacher's methods and habits and results. Missing is more than improbable. It is intentional.

George's reasoning quickly brought him to this: Ivan shot the nearby juniper snag on purpose. Ivan is watching.

George turns back in the direction of the concussion, his eyes searching the landscape for telltale movement, his heart rising with optimism about getting back to Ivan, and then getting back to the purpose of the weekend. He sees nothing at first. Then, some three hundred yards below, and beside a rock outcropping, a flick of something gray; a movement, set against the otherwise motionless, snow-covered ground, and in distinct contrast to the light snow still falling.

The gray thing is abstract at first. But with a little more movement it becomes less so, and George instantly knows he is seeing Ivan's gray plastic hat. He is seeing Ivan down there, stepping from behind the basalt, into full but distant view. George waves a big sweeping arm wave, and then begins hiking toward his best friend, not waiting to see if Ivan waves back.

"Crazy sonofabitch," says George to the snow. "Puttin' the lead that close. No wonder people talk about 'im."

George's boots make noise as he works his way a hundred yards closer, crunching through the snow and snapping things beneath the surface. Yet the snow muffles his steps, so it is easy to hear the air above his head being shredded by yet another passing bullet. And easier still when that bullet strikes the ground somewhere behind him. And when the blast from Ivan's rifle finally reaches him, George stops cold, stunned, not wanting to accept that his friend had fired again.

"Goddamn it!" George shouts down the basin. "What the fuck are you doin?! Goddamn it!"

Suddenly George faces a dilemma: stand in plain view to signal that he understands that Ivan is just messing around, or duck for cover out of instinct and a sense of self-defense, thereby signaling a new and unexpected truth, that Ivan is now an enemy.

George's feet stay put while he thinks, but he repeatedly turns from side to side at the hips, as if scanning the scene will somehow help him do the analysis.

"Keep your head, man," says George aloud to himself. "Keep your head and remember who you're dealing with here. This'll be alright. Another two hundred yards and the joke'll be over."

George stays in the open, throwing his faith behind the notion of genuine friendship, trusting Ivan despite growing anger over the foolishness of the moment. He begins walking again, directly toward Ivan. George raises up his right arm as far as he can reach and flips Ivan a proud and defiant bird.

"Fuck ya in the ass!" shouts George. "I'm comin' in."

George closes the distance between them with long strides and an energized pace, down to just a hundred yards or so—the same distance he and Ivan typically use to sight-in their rifles before the season. It's the same distance that, for purposes of shooting accuracy, Ivan is capable of placing five bullets through the same hole. At one hundred yards and looking through a riflescope, you can see a man's face, his breath, his disposition.

George Howard's disposition is not good, but he remains optimistic about how this will play out. Pissed, but hopeful.

George keeps his eyes on Ivan as he walks, on his friend's dark silhouette against the snow, which reveals Ivan's stance: legs spaced shoulder-width apart, one foot slightly ahead of the other, the .270 held diagonally across his mid-section, poised to shoot again.

George watches as Ivan lifts the rifle to his shoulder, snugging it in tight. George sees Ivan's gray hat tilt slightly downward to the action of the rifle. George thinks that if Ivan is going to take the game this far, maybe he should play along by diving for cover. But George is too angry to play along. He stays out in the open and keeps walking.

"You're just wastin' good ammo, asshole," says George in a loud voice that was not a shout. "And I'll be damned if you think I'm gonna share mine."

"Keep your ammo, asshole," replies Ivan in his own loud voice, now at a distance of just sixty yards. "I got plenty."

It strikes George that Ivan sounds different. He's heard the angry Ivan many times, and the insulted Ivan, and the taunting Ivan, too. The I-can-kick-your-ass Ivan is as familiar as fleas on a dog. The pull-the-wool-over-your-eyes Ivan is old stuff. The you-ain't-gonna-get-the-best-of-me Ivan is almost a cliché. But this man standing in the snow with a gun, this is a new Ivan. The oddity of this realization makes George slow his gate.

"What the hell, man?" says George, now just thirty yards away.

"Whadaya mean, what the hell?"

"Now goddamn it, you know what I mean," says George, still closing the distance. "Shootin' out there like that?! Ain't hardly the safest thing a fella might choose to do on a Sunday morning."

"Oh, Jesus!" exclaims Ivan. "The world is plum full of unsafe things. This ain't nothin'. And besides, don't you trust me?"

George now stands within fifteen yards, which feels close enough.

"Never had a reason not to," answers George.

"And now?"

"And now I think maybe you spent last night nursing on a bottle, so maybe you're a little worse for the wear this mornin'."

"That so."

"I'm thinkin' so."

"And I'm thinkin' ol' Ivan has had enough of your particular brand of bullshit," says Ivan. "I'm thinkin' maybe it's time you came clean with me. And stop playin' me for a fool. I ain't stupid, ya know."

"Oh I know," says George, choosing to humor his friend. "Never met a Thrower who was."

"Hmmph!," grunts Ivans as he absorbs the compliment.

"Maybe the smartest damn clan in the canyon, but—"

"But what?"

"But maybe not in a way most folks could tell, ya know?"

"Well I'll be go to hell," exclaims Ivan. "Here I am with a round in the chamber and the safety set to fire, and you're so confident about the situation that you're willin' to insult my family. Ain't you got balls."

"I ain't got no reason to worry 'bout that there .270," says George.

"You sure as hell do if you don't come clean with me."

Ivan stands steady for a moment. Then he lowers the muzzle of his rifle, aims for a spot between George's feet, and pulls the trigger.

Minute fractions of a moment in time become epochal.

Forty-five feet is a hideous distance for a bullet traveling four-thousand feet per second. Dirt explodes upward beneath George's crotch, simultaneously with the shock wave also coming from the muzzle of Ivan's rifle, and with the roar. George stands transfixed by the sight of the muzzle blast, the bright orange fireball that instantly mocked their friendship. George flies into the air, propelled by reflexes of a hundred muscles. George's rifle flies from his hands.

He gains very little altitude, and this fall back to earth is brutal. Because that descent lasts long enough for George to realize the gravity of things—the trouble he faces. He ends up sprawled on the ground, his back arching over a brittle shrub, his wide hands grasping wildly at the snow for control and reason.

An eternity passes during which the only available sound is two men breathing hard, and not in unison. Then Ivan finds words.

"Holy Christ! What's that smell!?"

George still cannot speak, but he also smells the foul but familiar smell. His own.

Ivan laughs as he returns his .270 to its resting position across his midsection.

"You know, ol' Georgy Boy, I'm a big believer in the recuperative powers of a good old-fashioned shit in the woods. But my God, man. You've taken it too far. Look at you!"

George's body shakes slightly as he maneuvers to regain his footing and composure. His lungs can only muster small, jagged breaths. He is soiled but not wounded. He is confused about Ivan and what's next, but sure of his own willingness to die if this is his place and time. George is always ready to die, and is secretly proud of that readiness. He searches for his next words, and then finds them.

"Shitty shot, deadeye."

The two men lock into each other's eyes, both still breathing hard.

"This can go one of two ways," continues George with sufficient resolve. "Either shoot me like you mean it, or empty your magazine onto the ground right now. Don't matter to me which way you go, but it's your call.

"You mean to say you ain't afraid of crazy ol' Ivan?"

"Hell, man. I'm afraid of pretty much everything in this motherfuckin' world. It's a long damn list. And all you've managed to do so far this morning is add your name to the bottom."

"Well I'll be go to hell."

"You and me both," says George.

The two men stand there in the snow, still panting steamed breath, stuck in one another's eyes, lost together in this new emotional landscape.

§

"Why'd you do that to me?" asks Ivan, now nearly in the voice of a child. "Why'd you make me think you were lost or hurt or dead out there?"

George does not reply.

"We were supposed to have s'more of them navy beans, you and me. We were supposed to sit by the fire and tell a few fine lies."

"I did."

"You sayin' you were there but I didn't see ya? Like I'm some sort of blind sonofabitch?"

"No, man. I'm sayin' I built me a fire out there. Kept myself company 'til the sun rose."

"But you were supposed to keep me company, weren't ya. And ya didn't, did ya?"

"And when I didn't make it back, you decided to keep company with Mr. Seagram's instead."

"What's the matter, man? Jealous?"

"And judgin' by the way things are goin' here this morning, I'd say you were up all night, just like me. Only while I was tryin' to stay warm, you were tryin' to stay drunk."

"What's it to you, Georgy?"

"Ain't nothin' to me, 'cept for the fact that for some goddamn reason you decided to start shootin' at me—the only goddamn person on this motherfuckn' planet who'll even put up with your crap."

"Right, and that's the goddamn point," says Ivan. "You're the only one."

§

George knows how it is when Ivan is drunk. He knows to make allowances. But standing there in the bitter morning air, smelling his own humanity and feeling all too mortal, George cannot predict the outcome of this. He'd seen Ivan Thrower do and say many strange things over the years, but none of it informs this rancid moment between them.

Ivan tries to reposition himself, his footing, but only manages to wobble a drunk's wobble. One foot slips out a bit on the snow before he catches himself and regains his confrontational posture.

"Easy there," says George, thinking of the .270.

"Easy yourself, asshole."

Their eyes lock again, both trying to divine an answer to this. Both wanting an out but unable to see it. George senses he has nothing to lose by pushing on anyway.

"You ever have a better friend than me?"

"Whadaya mean?" replies Ivan.

"I mean, anybody ever stuck by you the better than me? Ever been able to count on anyone the way you're able to count on me?"

The sudden change of expression on Ivan's face gives George his answer—that look of defeat.

"So what they hell are you doin' here?" continues George. "Drawin' down on me like this. Fuckin' with me like this. It makes no sense."

"You get yourself lost or something out here on Tumblejack. You don't make it back to camp. You leave me to spend the whole goddamn night to think the worst, thinkin' I might be drivin' outta here alone. And you want *me* to make sense?"

"Maybe that's askin' too much," offers George.

"Oh no, not you. It ain't your style to ask too much. 'Cause if you went around asking things of people, they wouldn't like you as much as they do. Oh, but they like you just fine. They like you a lot, and better than any one person deserves."

"Well if you think I'm so goddamn likeable, how comes we're doin' this horseshit right now?"

"Up and down the damn canyon, it's all I ever hear: what a good guy that George Howard is," says Ivan. "How'd I ever manage to buddy up with the likes of him? With George bein' so pleasant and all, and you bein' the way you are…"

"Answer my question," says George.

"What?!"

"Why the fuck are we doin' this dance; you with a gun and me with shit runnin' down my leg?"

Ivan takes a few seconds to collect his hazy thoughts.

"Because there ain't nothin' wrong with you. That's why. And because you got yourself a wife, and you don't even care about keepin' her. Because I got nothin'."

"I can't read," counters George.

"No, it's true, you ain't much for books, are ya? And a normal man, he'd make the most out of such a thing. A normal man would use that kind of drawback as an excuse for all sorts of bad behavior—drinkin' and carousin' and chasin' around. But not you! You're too goddamn good for that."

"I'm not so sure I'm good for much at all right now."

"Maybe not, Georgy boy."

"So looky here: since you say I'm too good for my own good, and it don't appear we're any sort of friends at all, how's about you just go ahead just squeeze off another round. Only this time don't fool around shootin' holes in the snow, Ivan. Just go ahead. Put one here in the ol' bread basket," says George as he points to his own belly. "I had me a good night by the fire. I've seen all I care to see of this dumbass life anyway. So why don't you quit pissin' and moanin' and just pull the goddamn trigger."

"STOP TELLIN' ME WHAT TO DO!"

"Go on, man. Make us both famous."

"SHUT UP!"

"No, this will be a helluva story. We'll be the two sorry sonsabitches who both wanted to be more like the other, right? But you got drunk and I got shot. Only thing we need is some wordy bastard to write it up. I'll be dead and you'll be pathetic, which is pretty much the same thing. So we'll be all square."

"GODDAMNIT, GEORGE!"

"C'mon, chickenshit. I don't care about goin' back to that goddamn canyon anyway. Shoot!"

Ivan swings the .270 back onto George, onto his belly, trembling. He looks George straight in the eye. He fires.

§

The roar both men hear comes not from the fierce muzzle blast of the powerful deer rifle, but from the metal-on-metal click of the firing pin hitting hard against the back of an empty chamber. There is no bullet. Ivan already fired them all. But the gun roared nonetheless, because that futile click tells the world what Ivan meant to do.

Then there is silence, save for the way wind comes up through the snow-covered sage, laughing at Ivan's futility.

Every little thing. Every rock. Every blade of dead grass. Every flake of fallen snow. Every gnarled juniper. Every creature on the ground and in the air. Everything mocked the misbegotten man who surrendered his dignity by curling his trigger finger against the fingernail moon of metal.

Yet this mockery is not the true price of Ivan's act. Only George Howard can exact that, and they both know it in an instant.

George takes one step toward Ivan, and that step shakes the earth.

George takes another step, and again the ground beneath them trembles.

Another step. Another shockwave below, accompanied by the sound of a freight train approaching from the distance, supporting George with a surreal intensity.

George's right hand becomes a fist. The skin draws tight across his knuckles, pushing the surface blood away from the boniest parts from this, now his weapon. George's right arm bends at the elbow and draws back. His shoulder and biceps muscles become ice hard. And all the while, the ground beneath shifts and flinches.

George shakes his head in disgust as he completes the set up of his punch from a distance of no more than three feet. Ivan makes no attempt to avoid what is coming. Rather, he just stands there with the look in his eyes of a child who cannot comprehend. The ground shakes hard, pushing George just that much closer to unleashing what promises to be the most punishing of blows.

But…

The reflex of muscles and retribution do not deliver—George's fist relents.

"Aw, Christ!" says George.

With that, George's right leg kicks forward and up, catching Ivan squarely in the crotch. Ivan goes down and the trembling earth receives him. It is over.

George picks up the two rifles from the snow and heads back to camp, following Ivan's footprints. He builds a morning fire big enough to burn the pants he'd never wear again. He warms water to clean himself up. Then he changes into fresher clothes and begins breaking down the camp, packing it away into the Club Wagon.

By the time Ivan finally shows up in camp, there is nothing left to do but leave.

"I'm driving," says George.

"What about the huntin'?" mumbles Ivan in a slur.

"We got skunked. That's all anybody needs to know."

Ivan shrugs his shoulders in drunken resignation as he moves closer to the Club Wagon. He leans hard against the front fender, fumbles to open his pants, and takes a leak. George takes one last look around the camp for remnants of their outing. But both men know in their guts that this biggest piece of debris is the trust that had always existed between them.

They get into the station wagon, symbolically picking it up together, this trampled trust. Neither man knows what to expect from this point, but wisdom and necessity suggest that the long drive back to the North Santiam Canyon is as good an alternative as any right now, George at the wheel and Ivan sleeping it off, or pretending as much.

It is a silent drive home.

§

Twenty-three years pass with the constancy and persistence of the North Santiam River itself. George and Ivan are carried along with the current of life, each man being taken through his respective set of rapids and channels and churns, moving faster than they'd like toward the uncertainty of what awaits when a river is no longer a river—when life as they know it no longer lingers on the distant downstream horizon, no longer promising a whole lot more to come. Both men gain wisdom along the way, but neither has any degree of certitude about what to do with it. Yet they both try to make it count for something.

Ivan now lives 330 driving miles from the canyon, in Mt. Shasta, California, the hometown of the woman he met and married about five years after that day on Tumblejack Mountain. George and his wife come for a visit, or more precisely to say good-bye to a dying Ivan—his life of smoking unfiltered cigarettes now in question.

The two women watch in quiet reverence from the doorway to the kitchen as the final act of friendship plays out in the living room, which is dominated by a rented hospital bed. Late morning sunlight filters through the windows with a soft diffusion that falls gently across the armchair where Ivan sits, having mustered the will and faint strength to leave bed one last time in honor of George.

That effort—along with the morphine—consumes what remains of Ivan's vigor, rendering him less able than he prefers to carry on a conversation of any consequence. But these men need few words. They only need this time together—George in a squeaky wooden chair borrowed from the back porch, now positioned so near to Ivan that the visitor can take the hand of the host, like an unflappable man of the cloth, steady in the moment, prepared to take what comes. Ivan's eyelids cannot hold their own weight. His head rests against the back of the armchair, and slightly to the right. George sits alongside, motionless, for nearly an hour, holding Ivan's hand. Their insightful wives step back into the kitchen, understanding full well that their time to offer quiet comfort is coming soon enough.

The morning light is already different when Ivan awakens with drifty, gossamer eyes, now looking upward toward nothing in particular.

"Where'd you go?" asks George.

Ivan tries to answer but his vocal cords respond with an unsatisfying threadiness. He clears his throat as best he can and tries again.

"Back by the creek."

"Tell me about that creek, Ivan."

"When Daddy's drunk, I go back by the creek."

"You like that creek."

"Momma called it my creek."

"Huh," says George with subtle appreciation. "Ivan's creek."

"Ivan's creek," repeats Ivan in a voice returning to faintness.

"And your momma knew."

"Momma knew…"

Ivan drifts away again, likely back to what George supposes is a childhood memory of a creek that served as sanctuary for Ivan, the bewildered, young son of a hard-drinking father. The topic had come up before. George understands.

A handful of minutes pass before Ivan awakens once again, this time with an unusually polite and complete question for George.

"I don't mean to make you uncomfortable," prefaces Ivan. "But is it going to hurt?"

"Is what going to hurt?"

"Dying. Do you think it hurts?"

George still holds Ivan's hand on the arm of the chair as he takes a few seconds to consider his answer.

"No, no. They say it doesn't hurt at all."

"Oh, okay," says Ivan, who seems to take his friend's word for it, giving him the comfort to drift away once again.

George hears the women in the kitchen, and realizes he is cramping up from sitting in that precise position for such a long time. He slips his hand free of Ivan's, which is now slack. He rises from his noisy wooden chair and scans the room, assessing things. That small sound brings the women back into the doorway to see what might be next. George first locks eyes with his wife, whose look of calm strength bolsters him. Then he shifts into the eyes of Ivan's wife and gestures with his arms to ask her a question. She nods her approval.

With that, George lifts and moves his wooden chair aside. Then he comes in close to Ivan, bending down to work his right arm behind Ivan's now boney shoulders and neck, and then his other arm beneath the Ivan's bent knees. He lifts his nearly weightless buddy, rising to a full standing posture with no indication of effort or difficulty.

George navigates the few steps from the armchair to the hospital bed, which faces toward the largest window in the room and away from the television that no longer means much to Ivan.

They look closely at one another—brown eyes into blue eyes and then back again—as George lowers Ivan onto the sheets and pillows. Neither utters a word.

An Important Storm

The weary-eyed men of the Mill City Volunteer Fire Department chose Kenny Hoyle as their chief, partly as a way to dodge the bullet of responsibility that could have just as easily taken aim on any of them. They elected him from their ranks on an unusually hot June evening—the only agenda item for their first-Tuesday-of-the-month Firemen's Meeting.

Then the assembled volunteers retired from the bare light bulbs, stifling attic air, and metal folding chairs that dominated the upstairs of their white, two-story firehouse to the relative comfort and evening air of the driveway out front. Here, with the red firehouse doors open to show the world their two magnificent fire trucks and their aging ambulance, the volunteers shifted back to being a bunch of guys hanging out after work.

A case of ice-cold beer in brown stubby bottles became the center of attention, procured from the back of the cooler at nearby Martin's Grocery. The men continued to convince one another between sips and belches that Kenny was the right choice.

Kenny's very first official decision came just days after that election, and it disgruntled old man Martin, who'd been trying to sell his store for three years. The new chief put a stop to beer consumption out in front of the firehouse, explaining to his thirsty constituents that the public might be more likely to donate money if the firemen of Mill City weren't seen polishing off beers as they polished their fire trucks. The men couldn't argue with Chief Kenny's logic, but the action left a few of them quietly second-guessing their vote.

Still, the men followed Kenny's lead, understanding in their respective private thoughts that people might also cut the volunteers more slack should they ever fail to save a house or a life.

He'd certainly seemed right for the job. After all, Kenny Hoyle lived just four blocks from the firehouse. And in his five years with the volunteers, he'd never failed to answer an alarm. He drove a narrow-box '48 Ford pickup with a white cab and dull red fenders that matched the color scheme of the firehouse. And though he was among the most aggressive firefighters in the face of flame and danger, he'd successfully managed to avoid even the slightest form of personal injury, which suggested that he was either smart or lucky or a little of both. These simple qualities were much admired and lightly discussed by those who voted him chief.

The firemen sensed Kenny could take the heat of leadership. What they didn't know, however, was that Kenny was a Renaissance man in hiding.

His Bachelor's degree hid in his sock drawer. His law degree hung alongside screwdrivers and wrenches in the garage. And even though people knew he was a lay minister in the Canyon Baptist Church, and a skilled chalk caricature artist who was popular at church socials and special events at the elementary school, they had no clue to the true nature of his life's path.

Kenny didn't come off as worldly. He had the classic look of a canyon man who worked too much and played too little. He was lean and rangy, with short, bristly, brown hair on a suntanned head. His frequently unshaven face was stoic, with constant creases born of genuine concern about events going on around him. His pale blue eyes reflected equal doses of critique and compassion. People speculated about him, that he might be hard to live with, but nobody really knew.

Kenny Hoyle took on the responsibilities of chief without becoming self-important—it was more a matter of paying off an old debt. Because back before he bought his own home, when Kenny's young family lived in one of the squalid rental houses owned by one of the few prosperous men in town, this same fire department showed up at the Hoyle's in the wee hours to skillfully subdue a frightening flue fire that had awakened his needy wife and two young daughters with a harrowing roar that none of them would ever forget.

Those same two beautiful red firetrucks had pulled into the Hoyle's driveway, followed by a half dozen private vehicles, each equipped with glowing red emergency lights fixed behind their otherwise normal looking front grills. Many of these same men had swarmed the roaring chimney like angry bees, some of them in pajama tops, all of them intent on doing a good deed. For Kenny, the time had come for him to also do some good.

§

Brenda Hoyle didn't like it when her husband told her of his desire to become fire chief the week before the vote. She sat on the edge of their bed, motionless in the hot evening air, surrounded by tired green wallpaper with pink roses in vertical rows, staring at her broken down house slippers for endless minutes as she absorbed his words.

Kenny leaned hard into the casing of their bedroom doorway.

She thought about how this was going to affect her. How she would have even less of his time and attention. How she was going to get stuck doing even more of the chores that go with maintaining a household. And how she'd have to settle just that many more squabbles between their daughters because now, in addition to daddy working long hours and extra shifts at the plywood mill, he'd also be missing in action at any given hour of what remains of his free time, off being the most responsible kind of volunteer fireman and—in her view—the least responsible kind of husband and father. By the time she looked up from her slippers, having completed her silent rant, Kenny had left the room. She spoke in a flat, emotionless voice.

"Do what you damn well please, selfish bastard."

That brought Kenny charging back through the doorway, now angry.

"Selfish!?"

"That's right," said Brenda. "It's what a fishmonger does. Sell fish!"

"Good Lord, Brenda. How can you say that?"

"Why? Just because you work your ass off? Just because you provide me and the girls with an above average house finally? Which by the way, is just barely above average."

"We do okay," said Kenny.

"Oh, like that's supposed to mean something to me."

"Are you saying it means nothing then? Really?"

Brenda started to laugh, but not in a way that signaled to Kenny that she might be softening. No, it was a laugh of pain peppered with sarcasm and disappointment, and it contorted Brenda's mouth into a clinching grimace that made her perfect teeth seem sinister.

"Listen, mister big shot fire chief. I'll tell you what would've meant something to me. It would've meant something if you'd turned out to be the man I thought I was marrying. It would've meant something if you'd become what you set out to become. Not this. Not just another guy working in a plywood mill."

"I hated being a lawyer. You know that."

"Oh that's right. I know the whole damn story by heart. Would you like me to recite it? Because I can."

"Not necessary," said Kenny as his eyes took a quick diversionary trip to the corner of the bedroom ceiling, and then back to Brenda.

"Goddamnit, Kenny. Is that where we are now? Doing only what's necessary? Is that as good as it gets now?"

"A lot of people would think that's good enough, because a lot of people can't even manage to get the necessary stuff done."

"Well look at me, Kenny. Do I look like a lot of people? Do I look like the sort of person who settles for what's necessary?"

She took his lack of a verbal reply as his answer.

"You're damn right I don't! And you know why?"

Brenda and Kenny locked eyes. The straight line of visual contact snapped the room into silence, because they both knew the unhappy answer.

Kenny broke off first, spinning on his heels in the doorway as if to leave once again, but then stopping—his hands on his narrow hips in frustration, his bristly head rolled rearward onto the thin flesh of the back of his neck, looking up into the nothingness of the hallway ceiling. Then he spoke with a different, quieter voice.

"If I wasn't doing this, I'd be dead by now."

Brenda giggled inappropriately.

"And my loving wife finds that funny," Kenny said to the ceiling.

"I used to be your loving wife, didn't I. Now I'm just your wife, and there's a big goddamn difference."

"And now she gets mean."

"Oh but wait! There's more! Because you've only seen the beginning of my mean. And after the way you've failed me, mister, you've got it coming."

Kenny started to leave yet again, instinctively wanting to get away from what he knew was next.

"Oh no, you don't get to walk away. You don't get to leave. Because if anybody's gonna leave, you can damn well bet it's gonna be me."

Kenny made it out to the living room, but stopped once again to shout back the only words that seemed available to him.

"I didn't become an alcoholic on purpose, ya know!"

"Oh, I know all right!" she shouted in return. "Just like you didn't mean to get a reprimand from the bar association. And you didn't mean to lose every last one of your clients. And you sure as hell didn't mean to lose so damn many cases. But you did it all, big shot."

Kenny reversed course, launching himself back down the hall and into the wallpapered bedroom.

"I've owned up to my mistakes," said Kenny resolutely.

"Ha!"

"Whadaya mean, ha!?"

"I mean bullshit, Kenny. I mean I was supposed to be married to a successful lawyer. I was supposed to live in a nice house in the hills of Salem or Portland or Eugene. I was supposed to have lots of interesting friends who do lots of interesting things and go interesting places. I was supposed to have a life, Kenny. But I don't, do I. All I have is this."

"You have what you have," said Kenny flatly. "You have us."

"Like that's supposed to do it for me? That's supposed to be enough? All that and a canyon, too?"

"It's enough for me."

"Wonderful! Congratulations on your big success! Someone call the Wall Street Journal, because I think I smell a story!"

Kenny glared at Brenda in anger.

"What? Too much sarcasm? Wish I could say I'm sorry."

Kenny growled behind his teeth. Spring-loaded muscles throughout his body twitched and sparked.

"Look at him. Two degrees, seven years of higher education, boxes of books he's read, smarter than any twenty men in this hellhole of a canyon, yet he can't find the words. Amazing."

Kenny had reached this crossroad of cross words before with Brenda, and he knew there was a decision to make: take the conflict up a notch and overwhelm her—typical of his drinking days—or take it down by retreating, leaving the final horrid words unsaid.

He chose the latter.

§

Kenny's daughters were among those who saw him, and the fire chief situation, in a more positive light. His youngest was dark-haired like him, and an industrious worker who rarely sassed and was very much looking forward to being a sixth grader in the fall. She was proud of everything Kenny did and was. His oldest was blonde and pretty like Brenda, but with a unique and transparent ornery streak that assured Kenny's acquaintance with every teacher and principal ever charged with watching over her in school, from kindergarten right on through to high school, where she would be a sophomore after summer. The older daughter wasn't so much proud of Kenny as she was glad to learn he'd be further occupied, and therefore a little less likely to monitor her every move. Still, she respected him. Perhaps because he cared enough to even try to keep an eye on her.

Kenny was also respected at the plywood mill, where he moved among the men comfortably. He held no more actual rank there than anybody else who'd been presented with a Simpson ten-year pin, but he performed one of the most prestigious jobs: day shift lathe operator.

The men of the mill had no choice but to physically look up to Kenny when he operated the lathe. Because, when his lanky arms and legs propelled him up the vertical steel ladder to the cab of the massive machine, and he took his seat inside the glass box, in front of its control panel with large colorful buttons, Kenny found himself several feet above the din of the main floor of the mill. It was Simpson's version of the royal box.

The mill could do no work until Kenny did his, which was to guide the giant, moaning mechanism in picking up ominous evergreen logs—they called them blocks—that had been cut to a length of eight feet and then freed of their bark. Kenny's machine snatched one log at a time with hydraulic arms of steel, heaving the block—still dripping with foul-smelling pond water—to a position where the lathe's spindles could be brought to bear at the very core of the helpless specimen.

Kenny's mechanized brute strength forced those spindles in deep, causing pond water and tree juice to ooze from the end cuts like a squeezed sponge. Then Kenny hit the button that set the lathe spinning and the mill working. The gargantuan chunk of nature turned slowly at first, like a child might spin an ear of corn by its end holders before deeming it ready to eat. But the revolutions quickly gained velocity per Kenny's instructions, until the block was a hurling blur, making its own wind and noise, spinning in place, in the grip of Kenny's lathe, angry but fearful about what was to come next: Kenny's blade.

It was a single, shining line of sharpened steel—Paul Bunyan's razor—perched at a height to match the spindles, creeping closer and closer to the mad mass of turning wood. And then, when Kenny said so, the blades took their first glancing swipes at the outer fringes of the whirling block.

Whoosh! Whooosh! Whooosh! Whoooooosh!

And with that, Kenny's lathe was fully engaged, peeling away relentlessly, diminishing the log by the second, unrolling it like so much toilet paper from a dispenser that would not stop, roaring like a waterfall during spring run-off, creating an eerie kind of harmony with the whining hydraulics of the great green lathe, producing an endless flow of veneer, which was instantly chopped crossways into random widths that fed onto wide belts running the length of a 75-foot table, enabling the men who lined either side of the fast-moving table to grab the pieces in graceful, fluid movements made dramatic by their ability to catch air under the veneer and float it like a crisp bed sheet, guiding its flight onto the wheeled bunker carts that lined the table that was kept busy by Kenny and his lathe, the men in a rhythmic lather, determined to keep up. Kenny made all this possible.

§

Kenny wondered about how it had gotten so hot on the day he became chief. He was puzzled, because that time of year in Oregon's North Santiam Canyon, cooler temperatures were normal. And rain was probable at least until the Fourth of July. But on that particular Tuesday, the big round thermometer atop Martin's Grocery hit 105° by four in the afternoon. The streets had begun to melt. Cars and trucks moving lethargically in the vicinity of the firehouse caused a constant crackle as tires popped tar bubbles oozing up from the pavement. *All this in June*, Kenny thought. *Must be some sort of sign*. "Maybe a bad one," he said to the steering wheel of his oxidized pickup as he set out to take the temperature at home.

He headed west from the firehouse. Kenny saw a flash in the oversized side-view mirror that hung out over his red running boards: lightning in the east, and thunderheads peaking up from behind the Cascade Range, trying to decide where to go next. They were towering thunderheads, with bright white tops illuminated by a setting but still dominating sun, the dark gray-blue bottoms beginning to show their anger along the high horizon created by the mountains. And lightning again. But no thunder yet. At least it wasn't detectable to Kenny's ear, because the guttural rumble of his flathead V-8 teamed with the whine of his transmission to fill his ears.

Kenny began willing the weather to come on in, to come home with him, because he knew it would help. Kenny and Brenda were still in love. But they could go long periods of time when one or both of them could forget that fact. And when that happened, things were bad.

Brenda would often speak only in monotones, if at all. Blonde daughter would do things to further damage her reputation. Dark-haired daughter would read. And Kenny would retreat to the detached one-car garage to invent work. He was a living portrait of a preoccupied, worried, wiry man with short brown hair that was butch-waxed to stand straight up from his tall forehead, which was creased from frowning at the task at hand, or at the chill in the house, or both.

But in this house, in this marriage, thunderstorms had special recuperative powers. Thunderstorms cured all, if only for the moment.

Kenny pulled the Ford onto the gravel of his own driveway, eager to silence the engine and listen. The pickup's door squawked as he opened it. The red running board squeaked mildly as he stood on it with both feet, wanting the few inches of extra altitude to look eastward above the trees, to listen with his eyes.

Perched there on the running boards, he remembered their first summer together. Their first Fourth of July, and the weather it brought, and what it all had come to mean.

§

That holiday was also a hot one. People were sweating by late morning, when Mill City's parade was forming up in the parking lot of the defunct sawmill that gave the town its name. They sweated even more as the parade inched down Main Street past Martin's Grocery. The old and the overweight took to the shade where it was available, fanning the air, chatting about how unusual it was to be so hot on the Fourth, because rain and ruined picnics were far more normal. But what nobody knew was that this particular Independence Day would cement a union between Kenny Hoyle and his girl.

They spent the whole day together. They watched the parade together. They each shared their admiration for the town's two beautiful fire trucks and its aging ambulance, which wore that same oxidized shade of red as Kenny's Ford. They wandered through the modest town carnival together, past the various concession stands set up to raise money for this cause and that.

Walking arm in arm, sometimes hand in hand, they greeted each other's friends and acquaintances as a couple, sending out a message to anyone who cared to pay attention. And with each step, Kenny felt himself becoming less awkward and more swept up by the blonde at his side. The one who smiled approvingly at almost everything he said and did that day. The one who wore white, ankle-length pants and a bright red sleeveless blouse made of bandana cloth, tied up short at the waist to reveal a portion of her flat, soft-looking belly. Kenny felt luckier and luckier to be with her as the day went on. He was increasingly distracted by his feelings for her.

Kenny felt fully reinvented by late afternoon, which coincided with the first pitch of the annual Fourth of July softball game between the Hilltop Meat Market team and a team from nearby Sublimity. He was as happy as he'd ever been.

The game went well past sunset, and then into extra innings because the teams had been so evenly matched: lots of big hitters on both sides, no sign of capable pitching on either side. The score was tied at 26 in the fifthteenth inning when the Hilltop Meat Market's catcher swatted a two-run homer that put fans and players out of their misery, setting the stage for the fireworks to come.

Kenny and Brenda barely noticed the teams picking up their bats and bases. They'd been sitting on a blanket just outside the first base foul line the whole game, talking in a close, quiet way that even the umpire had recognized as intimate.

Kenny and his future wife didn't really notice when the grass around them became more and more crowded by families and their respective blankets, anxious for the start of the fireworks. The couple could smell the pungent, lingering scents of smoke bombs and sparklers being lit all around them, but they sensed only each other. Sitting there on the blanket under the field lights. Talking. Smiling. Anticipating.

A fireman had ignited a highway flare far beyond the center field fence. He'd touched the intense, pink fire to the fuse of the first piece of fireworks, a single mortar that shot into the evening sky, exploding in a simple, single blast of pure white fire, echoing in the river canyon that framed the scene. The concussion had ended discussions all over the baseball field. All eyes had become fixed on the remnants of the first explosion, the falling embers.

The smallest of children had scrambled for the security of their family blankets, where their sitting fathers began rolling awkwardly to one side or the other to retrieve their wallets, understanding that before the fireworks would continue, the men of the Mill City Volunteer Fire Department would come through the blanket crowd, seeking donations to help defray costs for the next year's extravaganza.

A former high school football star turned overweight family man and volunteer fireman was the only one who actually interrupted Kenny and Brenda. He'd done so by placing his upside-down fireman's hat directly between the two.

"Folks?" he said politely.

Only when the real fireworks started did Kenny notice that the dark mountains to the east were decorated with thunderheads. And it was near the end of the show before Kenny realized that some of the bright flashes in the sky came from somewhere other than the firemen's launch site out beyond center field. By the time the firemen had ignited the standing frame that spelled out *GOOD NITE* in smoky white words, all of the blanket people realized that the fireworks on this particular Fourth would be continuing on in another form, and that it would be wise to gather up the kids and the blankets and make for their cars before things got *too* entertaining.

Kenny and Brenda joined in the excitement of the exodus, not so much because they cared about getting rained on, but because the energy of the moment played right into their own sustained excitement: like kids huddling beneath a railroad trestle as a freight train roars over them, at first resisting the urge to run from the cacophony of the monstrous diesel engines, but then running like hell, their hearts pounding, their mouths wide open, their hearts afire.

That excitement. That certain sense of something in the air. That's the kind of invigorating energy that engulfed Kenny and his closest-ever companion.

When they finally made their way through the crowd, he opened the passenger door of his then-new red and white Ford pickup and then helped her step up onto the running board, guiding her to slide in on the brown bench seat. She situated herself in the very center of the bench seat, her legs straddling the stick shift, before Kenny had time to enter from his driver's side door. The Ford itself had seemed happy as it roared awake and took them away.

The future Mr. and Mrs. Kenny Hoyle were parked in the darkness of what was once a sawmill by the time most people had made it home to bed. The abandoned mill was perched just high enough on the south wall of the river canyon to make them feel at an advantage. No buildings remained. There were only towering piles of forgotten sawdust that rendered their parking spot invisible from the road, giving them time to scramble should they be alerted by approaching headlights.

The late night air was still, warm and heavy. Their day had been all but perfect. Their future had begun to emerge. The stick shift was secured in the third gear position, as far forward as possible from the brown bench seat of the pickup. And as the thunderstorm drew nearer and nearer, gathering itself together after the hours-long struggle to breach the Cascade Range, crawling toward Mill City and the empty baseball field and the houses with their sleeping children, so did Kenny and Brenda draw nearer to each another.

Lightning now illuminated the night. Then thunder joined in the commotion, adding to the energy, the tension, the realization that the chronologies of their respective lives were gaining a new point of reference that would be shared between them from that night forward. The time between lightning flashes and corresponding claps of thunder reduced to nothing, as did the space between Kenny's face and hers.

The first drop of rain to fall near them did so quietly. Discreetly. But the rest of the raindrops were already on their way down. They all fell together. Dedicated to descent. Large and wet. Without a suggestion of restraint. Some raindrops were content to splash on the warm steel of the hood, or on the narrow wooden slats of the pickup's bed. Others landed on the rounded white roof of the pickup's cab, which shielded the couple from the weather but not from each other.

The luckiest raindrops were the ones that somehow managed to find their way to the precise spot on the face of the earth where two pairs of bare feet and naked legs extended from the open passenger door of a red and white pickup parked in the dark, striking flesh but failing to distract attention from what was happening on the brown bench seat. It was an important storm....

§

Kenny stepped down from the running board, crunching his boots into the gravel of his driveway. He was reluctant to go inside. He chose instead to stand halfway between his truck and the back steps, looking up at the evening sky, searching for clues that would help him solve the puzzle that vexed him, speaking incomplete thoughts to his long-dead grandmother, who he always imagined was up there, hearing him, offering him silent advice.

The clouds were not coming fast enough. The thunderstorm was also feeling reluctant, he thought to himself. "Coward," he said to the eastern horizon as he moved toward the back door, bracing to go it alone.

Kenny stepped inside and sat down on the back porch chair to unlace his work boots, as was his routine. The old wooden chair announced his arrival with a reassuring creak of wood on wood, letting everyone inside know that Kenny was home and ready to hear about their respective days. Ready to offer details of his own. But no one called for Kenny from the other room. No one acknowledged his arrival.

His gray wool socks carried him across the shiny linoleum of the kitchen. It was still. The light over the sink was off, which was peculiar because that light was almost always on, his family's version of a candle in the window, signaling that all's well. He reached up to pull the chain on the fixture over the sink, absentmindedly glancing out the kitchen window to the weather, wondering why there was no sign of supper as his hand felt the rhythmic resistance of the chain sliding against the white porcelain fixture.

Kenny turned from the sink and the light and the window to look past the kitchen table, which was clean and barren, through the arched passage into the living room. There were no lights on in there either. He walked into the still life that was his own living room. Motionless furniture. No signs of life. A cold television set. Two hammered metal plates on the wall, passing for art but looking more like fancy bronze cymbals. Plastic yellow roses in a vase on the bookcase. Dim light sulked in through the windows, but it was dull, gray, diffused light that served little purpose, other than to feed Kenny's confusion.

Kenny could hear his own heart beating in the solitude of his darkening house. A lone mosquito flew past his right ear, choosing not to bother with Kenny, its miniature wings sounding a subliminal buzz.

Those gray wool socks carried Kenny down the hall that led from the living room to the rest of the house: the bathroom, the two bedrooms, and the stairs to the attic. Only the bathroom door was open. But like the rest of the house, it was lit by the faint grays of the dying light outside.

Kenny reached for the dark brown doorknob to the room his girls shared. The door creaked open to reveal his dark-haired daughter, huddled by the window, using what light there was to read her Nancy Drew.

"Hi, Sugardove. Where is everybody?"

"Blondie's out with some new boy," she said without looking up. "Mom took off wearing her favorite dress."

"The blue one." he said sounding fatherly. "Where'd she go?"

"There's a note, Dad."

"You okay?"

"I'm fine. You better go read your note, though."

"Better turn on a light, so you don't ruin your eyes."

"I'm fine."

Kenny closed the door, and then turned to open his own bedroom door. Passing through the doorway where he previously stood to tell his wife about becoming fire chief, he hit the light switch. The overhead light was bright and harsh, causing Kenny to squint uncomfortably as he scanned the room for word from his wife.

There it was, on the corner of the neatly made bed. A small white envelope. Kenny snatched it up, flicked off the bedroom light, and headed back toward the light over the kitchen sink, which suddenly seemed like the safest place to be.

Dear Kenny, said the single piece of white notepaper in his hardened, uncertain hands.

Kenny leaned forward to rest his weight on the edge of the kitchen sink, just below his belt line, his whole body aimed to the east where the thunderstorm was supposed to have come from, hesitating to read on but then reading anyway.

I believe this is the first note I've ever written to you. Could it be?

Kenny nodded in agreement.

Anyway, this is my attempt at being philosophical. And I'm probably no good at it. But here goes.

Kenny unconsciously rubbed the bridge of his nose and simultaneously shifted his weight. The floor squeaked. The mosquito made a second pass at his right ear, an audience for his discomfort.

You're a very good man. You work hard. People respect you. You're honest and reliable. My parents love you, and my sisters envy me for having landed you. I've never known anyone braver.

Kenny, the grown man. Kenny, the husband. Kenny, the dad. Kenny, the lathe operator. Kenny, the volunteer fire chief. All of these versions of Kenny ran from the kitchen, scattering in all directions, leaving just one Kenny alone at the kitchen sink: authentic Kenny, a frightened boy.

I imagine that you'll handle this like you've handled every other difficulty in your life. I just know you will. And I know you'll find the right way to explain things to the girls.

The girls, he thought. What will become of the girls? What will we do?

You understand, don't you? You know that I've died inside. And that I can no longer see past the moment I'm in. You know there is no future. Not for us. Not for me.

Authentic Kenny trembled.

I know you know.

Dark-haired daughter appeared silently in the arch between the living room and the kitchen.

"Daddy?"

Kenny halted her advance without looking at her or speaking to her, by simply flashing the flat palm of his hand in her direction. She retreated.

You won't find me, Kenny. But God knows you'll try. Which is probably just another reason why you deserve better than me. You might not believe this, but sometimes I wish you weren't so good. Damn you, Kenny. Damn you.

"Sugar Dove?" Kenny called out in an emphatic voice.

"Yes, Daddy?" came a small voice from the back of the house.

"Go to the neighbors. Stay there 'til I come get you."

"But where are you—?"

"Go! Now!"

"But—"

"Now, please!"

Kenny leapt off the backporch steps, hitting the ground before the screen door could close, running for his pickup. The old Ford knew to fire immediately, backing out onto the side street beside his house, then surging up to the stop sign at corner. Right or left?

Left, answered Kenny's instinct.

Kenny headed west, his hands trembling on the steering wheel, his heart pounding, his prayer being that he was right about where to look for Brenda, and that he'd be in time.

Meanwhile, the thunderheads roiled over the mountains, trying to decide whether or not to come and help.

Brenda didn't get far or do anything bad the last time she left like this. She only made it a few miles away, pulling her black VW bug into the driveway of people she didn't know, distraught and confused. The woman of the house heard Brenda pull in and came outside to investigate. She talked Brenda down from her frenzy and took her inside to warm her with tea. The two women sat on a navy blue sofa and talked, the focus being that Brenda should head back home in spite of it all, which she did. The generous stranger never really understood the nature of Brenda's problem.

Kenny understood that this time was different. His worry was visceral, yet he remained able to reason probabilities through.

He knew she loved Meier & Frank, the biggest and finest department store in Salem, thirty-seven miles west. It was a shrine to Brenda's aspirations, he deduced. Rack after rack of things that announced and confirmed her taste and desired status. Proper sales ladies who seemed to recognize that Brenda was somehow particularly deserving of their courtesies. And mirrors. Brenda loved the mirrors, because no matter what she tried on or how dark her mood, those mirrors reflected her in the most flattering possible manner—young, beautiful, slim but shapely, intelligent, bound for better things.

Kenny drove Highway 22 into Salem, and then into downtown, arriving just as the Meier & Frank security man was in the process of locking the front doors. He leapt from his pickup and rushed across the sidewalk.

"Excuse me! Hang on there!" shouted Kenny.

"Help you, mister?" said the expressionless security man.

"Is anybody still in the store? Customers, I mean."

The security man turned his head from Kenny to look inside through the big glass doors.

"Just those women at the shoe register there. All of the other registers and doors got closed down already. You're looking for someone, I guess."

"My wife. Pretty blonde. About five-six."

"We get a lot of those, mister. Too many as far as my wife's concerned."

"It wouldn't have been that long ago," pressed Kenny. "Maybe an hour, hour and a half. Blue dress?"

That final clue sparked the security man's memory.

"Hey, you know? There was someone a little earlier. Trouble over in the evening wear section."

The look on Kenny's face said he wanted to know more.

"They had a woman get all upset because some other lady bought the dress she wanted. Raised hell and wouldn't leave it alone."

"A blonde in a blue dress?"

"That's right. Mad as a hornet and loud as a train."

"And she left?"

"I'm sorry to say, the store manager made sure of that."

Kenny hustled back to his pickup and took off for South Salem, toward the only other place he could think of to look. Toward the neighborhood Brenda coveted. The one they used to talk about moving to back when Kenny was a lawyer with prospects, and she was a woman with dreams.

Fairmount Hill.

Kenny's pickup did not drive comfortably or willingly on those steep, evening streets of prosperity. The engine was hesitant, and the clutch was disagreeable. But Kenny pushed on through the growing dark, driving slowly among the Tudor cottages that flanked the forested hillside, and then the big-porched Craftsman homes atop the hill, their windows aglow with warm interior lights that illuminated happier lives. He shifted back and forth between second gear and third gear as he prowled among the towering firs that predated every residence, hoping to catch a glimpse of her black VW. Hoping for a chance…

Suddenly, he saw a glint of something.

It flashed in the corner of Kenny's eye, from the direction of a dead end street going off to the right. One that reached to the very top of the hill, to the very precipice of wealth, where discreet driveways curled off into the landscaping and trees.

Peripheral light from Kenny's headlights reflected off of the chrome, rear bumper of Brenda's VW. Kenny stopped hard, jammed the gearbox into reverse to back up, and then pulled in right behind her car.

The VW was running.

Kenny saw a pale blue garden hose on the ground beneath the chrome bumper, connected to one of the two twin tweetybird tailpipes of the VW. It snaked on the ground toward the front of the car and then up through the open wing window on the driver's side. Right into the car.

Fractions of seconds crept by like centuries as authentic Kenny shot toward her door. He all but pulled the door off its hinges as his mind raced: *I can't see! Is she slumped over in the shadow created by my headlights? Am I too late?*

His frantic hands searched the interior for truth. His fingers and palms felt the seats and floorboard, reporting nothing back. No Brenda.

Kenny backed out of the VW and stood up straight, confounded, breathing as if the air was instantly thin, struggling to understand what she did, where she was. His heart strobed between fear and resentment over this ploy, her sickening game of threats.

He felt helpless as he stood alone among the homes of people who probably should have been his neighbors. Kenny's mind offered up the all too familiar declaration that served as his only consolation in such times: *never imagined my life would be like this.* And then, like a pure canyon echo, his vocal cords and lips and tongue repeated it.

"Never imagined my life would be like this."

"Like what?" said Brenda from off in the darkness.

Kenny's head snapped to direction of her voice.

"Brenda! Brenda, are you there?"

"Up here, having a picnic."

Kenny's eyes tried to zero in on her location, but his headlights were not aimed in the right direction. Still he realized she was in someone's yard, up behind what he could identify as the shape of a massive rhododendron. The blackness hid the specifics.

Then Brenda flicked her lighter and lit a cigarette. Kenny saw her, sitting there in her blue dress on an old blanket—probably the one she always kept in the VW—smoking in a stranger's manicured yard in the dark.

"Damn you, Kenny Hoyle," she said in a tone of defiance. "Damn you all to hell."

"Holy shit, Brenda," he said in resignation.

Kenny exhausted a huge breath, put his hands on his hips, and looked up into the treetops. The trees breathed back at him, having absorbed the advance winds of a thunderstorm that never arrived.

Those trees stood tall but not in judgment, seeming to understand the life he chose.

Nobody

Nobody told. At least not while the female county deputy was there in the dark and smoky lounge, responding to an anonymous report she felt should never have been phoned in. The caller said there was a disturbance inside the Spillway, two men were beating each other fiercely, and it was bloody.

The long Labor Day weekend had stretched into Tuesday for Deputy Vicky Hayden, who took control of the scene feeling disinclined to be anything other than the congenial constable. She was there to calm nerves with her sincere eyes and gap-toothed smile, write a quick report, and encourage a good night's sleep for all still in attendance.

The combatants had been hustled out before the deputy even arrived. One was ushered away by his brother, who had been his only friend in the Spillway when things got tense, and who was far better able to continue driving east on Highway 22 and over the Santiam Pass, toward counties where deputies wore different colors.

The other fighter was Andy Sawyer, who the deputy knew more intimately than anyone realized.

He was a local, a regular at the Spillway, and an emerging homebuilder when pressed to say what he used to be back in Southern California. He was also a husband to Maxine, whose idea it had been to move to Oregon after Andy's business tanked, and to sink everything they had left into buying the Viney Maple, an aging roadside restaurant in the North Santiam Canyon that she renamed Maxine's Viney Maple.

Maxine had wondered briefly about the wisdom of letting him go to the Spillway at all that Tuesday night. But her need to be alone, reading novels on the living room couch wearing the blouse of the day and underpants, was more powerful than any sense of duty tied to keeping a watchful eye over her troubled husband. She read instead. This was, after all, their routine: Maxine beneath a reading light in their living quarters upstairs from the restaurant, and Andy holding down one end of the bar in the shadows of the Spillway.

Her penalty for reading became clear when three patrons of The Spillway brought Andy to the back door of Maxine's Viney Maple, holding him tight against the handrails as Maxine scrambled to find some pants. Nobody spoke.

Once inside, she began washing blood off the face of a drunken man who was badly beaten and indifferent to cleaning up. Her mind escaped to a passage she had just read as she worked the washcloth hard on his face.

§

Andy grew up to become a handsome and athletic man. Although not tall, his curly brown hair and smooth tan skin combined with his bright, straight smile to make most women take notice, either out of attraction or envy.

He went directly from Newport Beach High School to the Navy. He saw the world from the decks of a missile cruiser. He earned the respect of fellow sailors by boxing anyone who dared in organized matches aboard ship. When his tour was up Andy returned home with a swagger to match his looks.

He was buying Milk Duds on a warm Saturday evening at a waterfront concession stand at Balboa Beach when he and Maxine first noticed one another.

Maxine and her short blonde hair grew up on the beaches of Southern California. She'd never been beautiful. Not even as an infant. As a 10-year-old, she was all knee socks and curiosity. As a teenager, she flattered every bathing suit she wore. And with each passing year she'd attained a degree of pluck, which combined with her startling intelligence to build her local reputation as a gifted and outgoing girl with wonderful prospects. She'd stood in aloof contrast to her parents, both of whom were closeted alcoholics who dueled nightly.

The Merit Scholarship program and San Diego State University had fallen all over itself in welcoming Maxine to life as a coed. She'd rewarded their confidence by holding down a spot on the dean's list without really ever studying; she had been much too busy on the beach, alone on a towel, devouring novels the way a fat tenor eats pasta.

Andy and Maxine had spent their first summer together making love wherever and whenever they pleased.

Since then, they'd both romanticized isolated images of each other from that summer, trying to hold onto them, increasingly less able to remember what it's like to fall for someone.

He still remembered her wearing a royal blue blouse that was unbuttoned just enough to be intriguing.

She remembered him on the beach in shiny swimming trunks, posing for invisible photographers. Nobody remembered much else.

Andy went on to build homes for Southern California's aerospace engineers. Maxine kept the books. They made money. They made friends, and worked hard at living the busy, go-go life they envisioned. And when time and energy permitted, they made love. But not quite like that first summer.

When the housing market cycled downward, it fell directly on Andy, knocking him out of his shoes and into the bottle. This coincided with Maxine's emergence as a fully accredited matriarch, capable of just about anything except helping Andy regain his self-worth. This was the circumstance when Maxine found the *L. A. Times* classified ad for a roadside restaurant in the western foothills of the Oregon Cascade Range. Andy went along with her scheme.

§

Finding a body floating face down in the water the Tuesday after Labor Day was no victory for Andy. He'd agreed to help when Chief Kenny from the volunteer fire department called that morning in search of searchers. He said yes because he figured he deserved a day of cruising along the shoreline is his small aluminum fishing boat, just his smoky blue Evinrude and his private thoughts to keep him company. Maxine liked the idea because it might be good PR for Maxine's Viney Maple—the owners being seen as good citizens and all.

He spent hours on the water that day. And he spent a good part of that time envisioning his eventual return to the boat ramp, looking weary and dismayed, having made the good effort and lamenting the grief of the surviving family. He imagined himself joining the other searchers on the floating dock, everyone agreeing that the whole affair was a damn shame and then going home to tell their versions of the day's events.

But when the curtain came down on the nifty canyon melodrama looping in Andy's imagination, he was alone on the stage. He was still alone in his boat. Nobody applauded.

The afternoon winds swept across the reservoir as they always did during late summer. They brought out the few remaining sailboats of the season and drove less hardy boaters back to their yellow jacket picnics on shore. But sails were not necessary to propel a human body through the water. This body, that of a young girl, found its way into an uninviting and obscure finger of water that reached back into what used to be a steep, tree-covered ravine. Andy nosed his boat into that spot precisely because he expected to find nothing.

But there it was, floating mostly beneath the surface.

The corpse.

It was ensnared in the long-dead roots of a fir tree stump. The tree had been cut years earlier when the Army Corp of Engineers brought Detroit Lake to full pool for the very first time.

Andy kept his distance for a good long while, aiming his boat into the wind, with just enough throttle to make certain he didn't drift toward the body even one second before he intended. He wondered whether to tie a line to the body and drag it out under power of propeller, or to maneuver the body free with his hands, or to simply leave the unsavory task of retrieval for others. Unable to decide and angry about having to make such a decision, his mind sought sanctuary.

He daydreamed, replaying his three favorite Navy boxing matches in order of occurrence, relishing the precision and power of each punch he'd landed, of every move he made to evade opposing swings. He was poetry. He was sweet. The ring was his world and he owned it. But no sooner had he reached the conclusion of this sustaining recollection than the reservoir winds served up a haymaker to the side of his boat: a punishing gust brought him fully about, ordering Andy to once again face the truth of the day.

And once again, he resisted. Andy maneuvered away and took the boat to the middle of the finger channel, still unwilling to answer the call. The wind died down, allowing him to go slack for a moment, and instantly opening the floodgates to yet another diversionary mental escape: he thought of Vicky Hayden and their first encounter. He thought of her brown eyes, and then details of the woman beneath the uniform—the small of her back in particular, and her natural scent—and this somehow revived his sense of duty.

The wind did not push Andy's boat back toward the corpse. Rather, he drifted back on his own accord, finally ready.

He hated being the one. And as he approached the bloated, softening flesh to do the job that needed doing, he spoke to Maxine, loudly and unreservedly.

"You self-absorbed bitch! You gotta-have-it-my-way piece a crap! Goddamnit I hate this. Goddamnit! And if it weren't for you, no way would it be *me* here doing *this*. No way! Do this, Andy. Fix that, Andy. Come over here and help me with this, Andy. Why didn't you think of *that*, Andy? I tell ya. Crazy peepshow bitch!"

Andy needed badly to be heard. But the floating corpse was uncooperative, insisting instead that it be liberated from the gnarly, waterlogged roots. Andy obliged, fulfilling his duty to Maxine, to the local authorities, and to a family of strangers who'd lost one of their own to the lake.

Afterward, Andy looked lost when he finally made his way into The Spillway Tavern, numbed by the day and bound for greater numbness. He took his regular spot at the end of the bar, where he often held court while his wife sat at home reading in her underpants. The bartender was host that evening to several people who knew Andy well, and two out-of-town brothers who didn't.

Beer flowed like the North Santiam River. Andy tried to re-conjure happy memories of sailors he'd pummeled, but that distraction failed. Then he tried to respark kinder thoughts about Vicky Hayden, but quickly realized it was neither the time nor the place.

His next best alternative became obvious within minutes—Andy found something about the larger of the two brothers he could mock, fired an insult across the bow of the man he wanted to challenge, and got the fight he desired.

Deputy Hayden had also spent that Tuesday searching for the body, all the while dreading the idea of possibly being the one. She entered The Spillway knowing full well that Andy was probably behind the trouble. More important to her on a personal level, however, was the knowledge that Andy had spared her from the unpleasantness of being the one. She was grateful to her secret friend.

Gas stations are rarely romantic. But for Andy and Vicky, the Flying A run by Roy Larimer became as much, because that's where they first made meaningful eye contact several months earlier, from opposite sides of the pump island. There was no conversation. No flirtations. Yet there was something inescapable: a vague resonance between them, the hint of a shared harmonic, along with a tingling sense that the longings of one might be fulfilled—at least a little—by the other. All of this was expressed through their eyes and nothing more. All of this required a response....

§

On the Friday after Andy found the body in the lake, Deputy Hayden stopped by Maxine's Viney Maple in the early part of her evening shift, hoping to get a sense of how Andy was holding up. The place was clean, well lit, and empty. Amber knotty pine encased the scene. Green vinyl booths lined the window wall, waiting for business. Maxine was behind the counter, busying herself in a way that betrayed her burning self-importance. The two women had never spoken before.

"Mrs. Sawyer," said the deputy as she straddled a stool at the counter.

"It's Maxine, deputy. Like the sign says outside. Coffee?"

Deputy Hayden nodded and grinned to acknowledge the permission, her girl-next-door easiness further disarming Maxine, who did not warrant that gap-toothed smile.

"Menu?"

"No thanks," said the deputy. "Maybe next time."

Maxine's body language suggested a mild resentment that coffee was the extent of the transaction, or at least that's what the deputy thought she detected. Maxine shot back into the kitchen area, and quickly returned with a fresh pie for the display case that sat directly in front of the deputy.

"Quite a difference from last weekend to this," said Deputy Hayden. "Traffic really drops off after Labor Day. Canyon really quiets down."

"Oh, I'm expecting regular weekend business," said Maxine with a tone of certitude. "It's just kind of early for the Friday dinner rush."

The deputy was surprised to realize how little Maxine understood about the seasonality of running a highway business in the canyon. She chose not to pursue the point, as her job forced the delivery of too much bad news as it was. She drank her coffee silently instead, waiting to ask the question that prompted the visit, but Maxine saved her the bother.

"You hear how my husband found that body up in the lake Tuesday afternoon?" said Maxine to the deputy from the length of the counter. "All those people up there searching, and it's my own Andy who gets the job done."

"Yes, we all heard about that," said Deputy Hayden. "Nasty business."

"Oh, no," said Maxine with a grin that showed how much she enjoyed her own irony. "I think it'll be real good for business. People can't stop talking about it. And some of them even want to shake his hand, because when a person finds a body, it kind of makes them a celebrity."

"For a week or two, I suppose," replied the deputy.

"I try to get him to come downstairs and be sociable with people, but ol' Andy, he's been shy this week."

"Hiding that shiner of his, I bet."

"Hmm," said Maxine with mild dismay. "So you heard about that, too."

"Goes with the job, ma'am. How's he doing?"

"My husband's just fine," said Maxine, who then came nearer to speak in a lower tone. "He's playing up this martyr stuff a bit too much for my taste, licking his wounds upstairs all week. But he's fine."

"I heard he took a pretty good lickin', though."

"He's had worse," said Maxine. "And it isn't anything compared to the beatings that get put on that little guy in Mill City they call Numbface."

"Shiner Black?"

"Yeah, that's the guy. Always picking fights with guys twice his size."

"Well, Shiner Black is one thing. But Mr. Sawyer, he was a Navy boxer wasn't he?" asked the deputy. "Knows his way around the ring, right?"

"That's…right," said Maxine with puzzled hesitation, instantly suspicious of the deputy knowing that detail about Andy.

"So how's it possible he could lose so badly to a stranger in The Spillway? No way he should have lost that fight."

Maxine leaned in closer still, as if to share a secret.

"Well, that's the thing about my Andy, and you can share this with your police friends. He only loses when he means to."

With that, Maxine spun away from the deputy and returned to the important chores of a restaurant proprietor. Deputy Hayden took another sip of coffee. Then she took a small notepad from her uniform's shirt pocket and grabbed a pen Maxine had left behind. It might have looked like the deputy was making important police notes. But in fact, she was adding another item to her personal grocery list, which she intended to fill at some point during her shift. She wrote down the words *Black Cherry Kool-Aid*. As she did, her mind wandered off in a familiar direction—to a mental lineup of men she encountered in the canyon, most she wouldn't have, a few she would but couldn't have.

She thought of the volunteer fire chief, Kenny Hoyle, whose simple smile suggested a complicated life. She thought of Shiner Black, and wondered whether her compassion might make the canyon's most self-destructive man a little less so. She thought, too, of Mike Davis, the married deputy who stirred feelings in her, whose by-the-book approach to life made it impossible for her to be anything more than a fellow cop.

She took another sip as her thoughts came back around to Andy—who once had nearly been her Andy. Her man. She thought how she might have been a better wife for Andy Sawyer than this Maxine, because she'd already been willing to try solving his mysteries and she'd already been willing to let him try to solve hers. She thought about how she and Andy briefly had plans to devise a kind of happiness. That way he wouldn't have to lose fights on purpose, and she wouldn't have to feign toughness.

But those truths ultimately could not be overcome by a liaison or a life with Andy, or any man, because they were too deeply entwined in her very essence. This much she knew for sure. That's why she ended it with him before it really got started. That's why she always ended up asking herself in the same soft, sad voice:

"Is this it for me?"

Those were the kind of nowhere thoughts people could have when they spent too much time sitting alone on bar stools in the North Santiam Canyon.

Nobody was exempt.

Pecking Order

Tom Kettle was a flawed man who, like most of us, appeared otherwise at first. But even the most unsympathetic observer would have to question whether he deserved what he got. After all, he was an intelligent man with two degrees and an artful sensibility. Although not tall, he was fit and handsome, with waves of red hair and a porcelain smile.

He was a decorated veteran of World War II, having copiloted B-17 bombers on twenty-three missions over Europe and then returned home to brag about it too much. He was also a natural athlete who, after the war, took full advantage of the GI Bill and his own competitive nature to become a twenty-seven-year-old walk-on basketball player at Central Washington College of Education in Ellensburg. He was a second-string guard with an unattractive, low to the ground sort of dribble and an even less attractive semi-jump shot that almost always went in. Opponents learned to hate Tom because he always smiled as he shot the ball. His teammates felt the same way, which explains why, given Tom's comparatively advanced age, he was derisively referred to as Pa Kettle—but only when he was out of earshot.

Tom came home from the war with more than the confidence that comes from cheating fate. He came home with a war bride.

A shy, round-faced, dark-haired Dutch girl, who, having been victimized by fear of the Nazis, instinctively fell victim to Tom's victorious American swagger. Her name was Ellen.

By the time Tom and Ellen settled into married student housing in Ellensburg, she was pregnant with the first of their two children. No sooner had she stopped nursing their daughter than she became pregnant with their son. Ellen's fate was cast. She spent the next few years changing diapers and chasing children and crying silently while they napped. And all the while, Tom pursued his personal ambitions, an oblivious warden to his wife.

Nobody came to say good-bye when, after earning his teaching degree and telling every boastful story he knew to anybody who'd listen in Ellensburg, Tom moved his unhappy family to Seattle. To a cramped apartment near Queen Anne High School, where he got a job teaching social studies.

Sometime between Thanksgiving and Christmas vacation during his third year at the chalkboard, Tom realized he'd made a mistake about teaching. It turned out to be too much work. And, while his students were a wonderful audience for his stories, it just wasn't all that he'd hoped for. So he began casting about for a new career. And by New Year's Day, he had his answer.

Advertising.

For a man with flyer's eyes, Tom continued to be remarkably unobservant about the conditions of the people around him. He was becoming increasingly self-absorbed and inattentive toward his wife, which explains why he did not notice that Ellen nearly dropped a bowl of mashed potatoes when informed that he was going back to college, to get an advertising degree from the University of Washington. He'd earn his second degree in short order, Tom explained, but only if he could go full-time and not be distracted by work. She would have to get a job to make ends meet while he worked toward this new goal. Ellen was staggered by the news, and smiling Tom simply missed it.

Ellen struggled with her English but was good with numbers. This allowed her to find work as a grocery store checker on Queen Anne Hill. Her paycheck bought oatmeal for the kids and tuition for Tom. He went to the U. District everyday, even when he didn't have classes. He met interesting new people, and cultivated various circles of friends with whom he could hold court. Sometimes it was in the student union. Sometimes it was in a tavern. Sometimes, when it wasn't damp, it was out on the lawn. But most of the time, it was in the halls of the School of Journalism. This was where Tom shined, because he'd quickly shown promise as an art director—crafting compelling print ad layouts in class, deftly finding his way with typeface design for headlines. Students and professors alike were strangely drawn to the persona Tom created for himself, and they all but flocked around him to see his latest efforts. Week by week, he became a star.

Ellen did not attend his second college graduation. She took her children to the zoo instead, which was fine with Tom, because it gave him just that much more freedom at the ceremony and subsequent parties to celebrate with his younger, more optimistic friends. Tom was all pomp. Ellen was stuck with a circumstance.

The money situation improved after that. Tom landed his first art director job at a reputable local advertising agency, where he worked on the Puget Power & Light account. Three years later he jumped ship to a bigger, more imperious agency. The clients were bigger and the budgets were fatter. Egocentric creative people did daily battle in those elitist halls with tight-ass account executives.

Tom landed comfortably in the middle of all that self-importance, and thrived for a good long while. He got to work on the most important accounts, and made the most of those opportunities by turning out a body of stylish work. He began winning awards in creative competitions. And much to his quiet delight, Tom managed to increase his stock at the agency without actually taking on any real responsibility. The turning point came when, after 13 years as the agency's top senior art director, he was featured on the front of the Living Section of the *Sunday Post-Intelligencer*. It was a story about Seattle's creative community. He was the aging poster boy.

It was around this time that Tom devolved into a complete affectation. His red hair was fading to a pale silver, prompting him to grow out this beard to mimic Hemingway. He began dressing like a British country gentleman, with a variety of heavy sweaters and bulky wool slacks that required exaggerated suspenders. Also, he bought three different styles of Barbour waxed cotton jackets in dark olive. He'd become a caricature of someone who seemed important but really wasn't. Younger creatives mocked him, usually behind his back and sometimes to his face. But the old man of the creative department was too preoccupied with art directing *himself* to realize that he'd become the official agency fool. He even went so far as to embrace the nickname his young compatriots had given him, believing it to be symbolic of his own everlasting youth. But *Tom Boy* was not a term of endearment for the man of tweed and pretense.

Tom continued on at the agency well past his prime, mainly because the agency founder hated firing people. His work became less and less original. His assignments were increasingly less important. But Tom changed with the times. He told himself that he'd earned the privilege of coming in late and going home early. And he was actually proud that he'd perfected the art of sitting at his drawing table with his back to the rest of the bustling office, his glass door closed, his elbows on the table, his head in his hands as if to ponder a creative challenge, facing out the window toward the tugs and ferries on Elliot Bay, sound asleep.

The end came when Tom, at age 56, engineered an out-of-town photo shoot for a small client that made and sold goose down comforters. He'd booked a Los Angeles fashion photographer. He'd selected a sensual-looking model from a stack of black-and-white glossies. He'd orchestrated a bedroom scene with a four-poster bed and mountains of goose down comforters. He'd instructed the photographer to be bold about showing skin, assuring everyone on the set that this was precisely what the client back in Seattle really wanted, and that this was going to sell goose down as never before. But, when Tom returned to the agency with prints that emphasized the model's most intimate attributes at the expense of the client's product, he was encouraged to retire.

Tom's daughter and son had long since grown and gone, forsaking their ridiculous father but staying in close contact with the resilient Ellen. She agreed with Tom's plan to leave Seattle for a small acreage in the North Santiam Canyon in the foothills of the Oregon Cascades, where he was born and raised. She was indifferent about his plan for a dual pursuit there; painting in oils, and raising chickens to produce eggs. And she was not at all distressed to realize that she no longer felt affection for the man. Then again, she'd been hiding a genuinely rewarding relationship for years—with a man who'd been a regular customer at the Queen Anne Hill grocery—which had been far easier than hiding from Hitler.

Tom proceeded as the chicken farmer artist.

He set up a chicken house to accommodate three hundred birds. He invested in automatic equipment to feed and water and collect eggs, believing these modern conveniences would allow him the time he needed to pursue his art, yet never mastering the operation of it all.

The only part of chicken farming he really liked was the morning ritual of walking among the cacophony of his subservient egg layers, smoking his pipe and inspecting his troops. He liked the sound his heavy boots made on the elevated wooden grating that was, for the chickens, the ground. And most of all, he liked to pick up a random bird and throw her high in the air, very near the ceiling. This was how he silenced the masses, because he knew that his chickens were instinctively afraid of any bird flying above them, recognizing it as a bird of prey. Two hundred and ninety-nine chickens would freeze in utter silence, each with its head cocked to one side, each with an eye fearfully trained on the dangerous bird above, each unsure what to do. Tom enjoyed that power.

This new life went on for seven months before Ellen got up her nerve. She slipped away from the house and left for good as Tom was conducting his morning chicken ritual. She drove her car down the winding and shoulderless road to the tiny town called Gates, turned left onto Highway 22 toward Salem, and eventually got on Interstate 5 heading north toward Seattle, toward her friend back on Queen Anne Hill.

It was a cool, gray Tuesday when she left Tom to walk among his chickens. His pipe smoke blended with the visible mist of his breath. The aroma of his dark cherry tobacco battled against the stench of the birds.

Well to the back of the chicken house, nearly to the point where he typically turned around to go back toward the door, the wooden grating gave way.

Tom's right leg shot downward to the solid concrete below and broke on impact. In that same instant, the spear-like end of one of the broken slats penetrated the inner thigh of that same unfortunate leg, coming to rest amid the muscles and tendons and fat, firmly against his femur. His pipe bounced away from him, spilling hot ash. The chickens froze in temporary silence, but this time they were not looking up.

Ellen was not there to hear him yell for help. Nor was anybody else.

Five days passed before another human set foot in Tom's chicken house. It was a county deputy, who'd been summoned by the neighbors down the road who'd detected a scent coming from the Kettle place that superceded the predictably acrid smell of chicken waste.

Deputy Vicky Hayden discovered dead chickens. About twenty, she figured. Laying here and there on the grating. Some of the dead remained intact. But several had been reduced to bone, beaks and feet. The deputy had grown up on a farm. She understood the scene.

The automatic feeding apparatus had gone haywire. The chickens had gone hungry, and that triggered their natural penchant toward cannibalism. Lacking adequate feed, they'd begun eating one another. That's how it works, reasoned Deputy Hayden.

It took a few moments for the deputy to notice the cluster of chickens in the rear. Curious, she walked slowly across the wooden grating. That's when she discovered what would quickly attract many more observers and investigators. It wasn't so much that Tom was dead. It was that Tom had become a feast for his own starving chickens. It was that he apparently laid there, stuck in the grating with a badly broken leg, unable to move and helpless to defend himself from the onslaught of sharp, pecking, omnivorous beaks. It was that he had been substantially reduced. It was that he paid a monstrous price for failing to properly maintain his automatic feeding equipment.

When Seattle police finally found Ellen on Queen Anne Hill and told her the news, she asked if they might excuse her briefly so she could call her children. First her daughter. Then her son. But in both instances, she began with the exact same words.

"He had it coming."

The Taverner Place

He did it the way I wanna do it. The way I hope to do it. Like a wise, old Indian. Or an animal that lived well and then knew by instinct which path to take to get out. He knew where to go and how to get there. Best of all, he sensed when it was time to go.

I envy him for that.

Brown Taverner lived alone in this house for as long as anybody can remember. They say in his later years, he didn't drive much at all. Only to town once a week to get supplies and whatnot. Toward the end he quit driving altogether. Otherwise, they say, he walked a lot. Up and down the road. Sometimes west toward town. Sometimes east into the woods.

I recall seeing him myself a time or two. Because years before we got the chance to move up here, I used to come out and drive this road just to clear my head. And to see if maybe someone had finally decided to put out a For Sale sign. It's not a strong memory. But I've got this image of an old, hunched-over man in overalls and a red-and-black mackinaw, with a saggy face. That musta been him. I like to think it was him. Gives me a stronger sense of the man whose house I now own.

Make my living as a butcher, I do. Built my business on sharp knives and honest cuts. People know the name Mike Hayden, and they look me up in the phone book when they need meat. Hayden Mobile Slaughter. My better half, Jen, she came up with a more creative name. "How about if we call it Vaganza Mobile Slaughter," she says. "You know, not quite an extravaganza, but still a pretty big deal. Get it?" I got it. But as the lettering on the side of my truck shows, I didn't really care for it.

Bought the Taverner place on the strength of people's taste for meat. Made the down payment right at the end of hunting season, when the business was cash rich. It's not the house Jen wanted. But it's all we could afford our first time out, and she did a good job of remaking it in her own way. I've always liked this place for its big front porch facing north, and its steep-pitched roof, and for the way it sits against the base of the foothills, back from the road some, with a year-round crick. Otherwise, it's just a white, two-story farmhouse that got built decades before I got built. Jen painted the shutters blue to freshen it up some, which I suspect woulda been okay with Taverner. I mean, he may be gone now and all, but I figure he oughta have a say about things like that. Seems only fair.

There was no family involved when the place went up for sale. Taverner had things set up with the bank or some trust company so it got sold automatically. Don't know who got the money. Don't really care.

Someone had been in to clean the place up before we took possession. But they didn't do all that good a job, seeing as they left quite a lot of Taverner's stuff scattered here and there. Who knows? Maybe they just flat out didn't know what to do with a lot of it. Maybe they just couldn't bring themselves to throw it all away. Maybe they took the really interesting stuff home with 'em when the boss wasn't looking. Maybe not. At any rate, traces of the old boy's life are everywhere.

Jen found his mismatched silverware in the kitchen, shoved in the back of a drawer. Most men don't care about silverware. Bachelors care less. But the one thing Taverner musta cared about was efficiency. Because even though the forks didn't go together, every one of them had sharpened tines; sure sign of a man who only wants to stab his meat once. No wasted motion for him.

She also found thirteen bottles of Old Spice on the top shelf in the bathroom. They were lined up all neat and straight, like sailors at attention. The tall-ship logo on each bottle was faced out toward the front, and rotated slightly to the left as you face 'em. Like the captain had given the *eyes right* order. Not a one of 'em had been opened.

"Whadaya suppose?" said Jen, who stood on the toilet seat to see.

"Hell if I know," I said, holding Jen at the waist to keep her from slipping. "Maybe he was a lady's man."

"Or maybe he hoped to be."

The fruit room revealed Taverner's knowledge of canning. By all appearances, he put up peaches and pears with genuine skill. Green beans, too. We found a few jars from what must have been his last season. Quart Mason jars, sealed up real good. We could tell by thumping the lids. It clearly wasn't the work of some kindly widow lady down the road, because the blue enamel canner was sitting right there on the floor, complete with the wire rack that steadies the jars in the boiling water. Looked like it'd been used fairly recently, and put away clean. We started enjoying the pears and beans and peaches right after we moved in last year, because we decided to trust Taverner's work.

Sometimes I sit on the front porch trying to imagine him. I look up at the mountains facing the house and think about how he musta done the same. How he mighta sat there with a cup of coffee, watching the clouds moving and swirling on the canyon winds, drifting into the mountaintops and squeezing through the trees, sweeping into draws and drainages and then curling back down onto themselves and starting over. Sometimes I wish I could see the wind currents in different colors, so I could track 'em better, and understand what was happening up there where the clouds meet the mountains. I bet Taverner did, too.

Twenty-some feet off the backporch, there's a doghouse under the apple tree. Its roofline matches the big house, with the same steep pitch. The siding matches, too. And judging by the patch of bare dirt right in front of the doghouse, Taverner musta had a medium-sized dog. There's black and white fur snagged on a nail that tells me it was most likely a Border Collie. One of those smart but loyal breeds that sticks close. The hand-carved nameplate above the little doorway reads "Suzy". I imagine Taverner enjoyed his Suzy quite a bit. I imagine they were close. Because from what I've heard, they left on the same day.

Suzy musta been free to roam the place. Her tracks are still plain as day in the red dirt floors of the out buildings. It's fine dry dirt that's been sheltered from the rain for decades, and ground down by Taverner's boots for just as long. The kind of dirt you wanna draw pictures in. In a few places, you can see Taverner's boot prints. Size nine or so by my guess, which goes with my memory of Taverner walking in his mackinaw; a man of medium height and build.

Even the dirt floor of the old pump house remains dry. It's a small shed made of red masonry blocks. The well inside still produces water that's sweet and pure as anything, which is mostly what convinced Jen that we should go ahead and buy the place. "If the water's good," she said to me, "the rest will follow." That was her way of saying she was okay with buying the place.

At some point Taverner put in a good electric pump to bring water up from below. But right beside the new pump sits the old one—a hand pump painted orange. And hanging from a hook right above is Taverner's tin cup. White enamel, and all chipped up. First time I saw it there, I got a vision of the old boy stopping by his pump house to fill that cup with water he pumped by hand. I could see him tipping his head back to get every last drop, his free hand planted on his hipbone. I could hear him slurping it down real loud, and then letting out a great big "ahhhh" for Suzy. Always irritated Jen when I made that sound. But out in the pump house, with Taverner's tin cup, I get away with it.

The biggest shed out back is basically a long garage, or maybe what you'd call a very small barn. Anyway, the end facing the house has double doors that open up to a dirt floor that's big enough for one rig. Yet that parking area inside accounts for only a third of the floor space. The rest is an elevated plank floor. And running the length of the building against the far wall is a damn fine workbench. One that's stout as hell.

This is where I suspect Taverner was happiest. The tools musta been recognized for their value and cleaned out in total, but there was no hiding what went on out there under that corrugated metal roof. He made stuff. He fixed things.

The workbench is lit by three light bulbs hanging down from bell-shaped fixtures. Down on the one end of the bench there are motor oil stains; you can still smell the oil. Four evenly spaced holes in the top of the bench show where Taverner had his vise; its footprint is the cleanest spot. On the floor below the vise, metal shavings twinkle.

The other end of the bench was for woodworking. It's cleaner and friendlier. Just a few specks of paint and varnish, and a buncha accidental drill holes and saw marks. The only window in the place is right in that same spot, so I figure Taverner did his trickier projects there for the extra light.

I've been spending time back there in Taverner's hangout, because the way I see it, a fella's not gonna come across a place like this very often in his life. A place that makes you feel good. So it's best to take advantage of it while you can. Because you just never know when things are gonna up and change on you, and you may never get another chance to, I dunno, have some place where you can work on the things that eat at you. Maybe get things right in your head. A place where you can cuss out loud without bothering anybody. Talk to yourself without looking like a damned idiot. I do all these things out at the workbench in the back of the barn. I'm lucky for it.

The studs in the wall behind the workbench are exposed. Taverner put sections of two-by-four between the studs to make little shelves, mostly for nails and screws and whatnot.

The people who cleaned out the tools musta had little use for all of those bits and pieces, so they left it behind. Fine with me, because you can never really have too much variety.

I went through every tin can and baby food jar to see what I'd inherited from the old boy. Spent a whole Saturday afternoon just picking through it all, reorganizing things. Right up to suppertime. And just before Jen hollered off the backporch for me to come wash up, I found a piece of white paper in a can of finish nails. It was folded up tight and small, with rounded corners that reminded me of river rock. Used my pocketknife to pry up one corner, then I was able to unfold it without wrecking it. It was a note written in blue ink. In a woman's hand.

Dear Brown,

Don't write. Don't call. Don't try. That's all.

Yours Truly,

Hattie

Can't really say why it is that I never told Jen about the note, or even considered chasing down the mystery of this Hattie. Except for the fact that it's Taverner's truly personal business, and that maybe I just don't feel it's my place to go digging quite that deep into his private life without his permission, which I can't get.

I put the note back. Same can. Same spot on the shelf. The way Taverner left it.

Living in the foothills of this Oregon river canyon suits me fine. I'm pretty sure Jen would say the same except for the isolation. She was good about it, though. Made the best of things, like almost always. Applesauce out of rotting apples, you might say. Then again, Jen was never the sort to do anything against her will, and she sure as hell woulda never married me if she didn't have her reasons. I'm just lucky she found me tolerable.

A damn sight luckier than Brown Taverner, who couldn't get his Hattie to come closer. I hope there were days when he felt lucky, too. I 'specially hope he felt lucky on his last day, because he truly was. Hope he had the sense to realize it.

There's not too much that riled Jen. But when I got to talking about how Taverner came to his natural end, there's no mistaking how she felt. Because, she said, it's a completely selfish thing to do. And it would be torture for her if I did the same.

But of all the things I like about Brown Taverner, I admire him most for having the balls to do as he saw fit. If I have half a chance when my time comes, I want to do the same.

I always hoped that if Jen outlived me, she'd learn to forgive me.

Cuss me.

Then forgive me.

I know which path he took. It's an old game trail that takes off up the grassy hillside that rises behind the small barn. Deer use it to come down out of the hills at night to feed in the fields and drink from the crick. The trail angles across the hillside and heads directly into the timber that stands tall above our place. Inside the forest, the trail wanders through the trees and the viney maples and the rotten logs and the bear grass, rising every step of the way. Approaching the ridge top from deep inside the woods, you start to see sky between the trees. Then before you know it, you're out of the woods and back in the open.

They say it was a Tuesday in October when Taverner and Suzy took off from the house, never to be seen again. That's the part that makes me grin. Because old as he was, Taverner did a darn good job getting himself someplace where nobody could pester him. A fine final effort. And if I ever got the chance, I'd like to tell him so.

The way I see it, Taverner left the trail once he crested the ridge and found the sun. He musta moved along the ridge, picking his way among the big gray boulders and the tall dry grass and the madronas and the maples. He likely found a spot that suited him, and just sat down with his back against the trunk of a tree, with his bony ol' legs comfortably out in front of him, his face feeling the warmth of October sun on the one side, and the coolness of October shade on the other. Figure he sat there with Suzy for hours, remembering the good things and letting go of his regrets. And then, with the sun getting lower, he musta drifted off to sleep. And by the time the sun got set, his breathing musta got short and shallow. Finally, just as the evening star showed up, I figure he took a couple a quick breaths and then let 'em both out together. And that, by God, was that. Fit and proper.

Yes, Jen thought it was cruel of Taverner to leave himself out there for somebody else to find one day. I tried to explain to her that the old boy had it figured about right. That for him, dying in the hills was a helluva lot better than dying on the bathroom floor or in a rest home or at the hospital. That he knew he'd eventually be found by hunters soon enough, and that hunters are, for the most part, folks who can deal with the shock of finding a body in the woods. That a lot of them half expect this sort of thing. That most folks in this damn canyon have a way of putting bad experiences in places where they'll do no further harm. Same way my kid sister—the county deputy—goes about doing the nasty parts of her job. Same way I run my butcher shop, not letting myself think about the meat as a critter that I coulda been friends with. So it's really not all that bad. Not like you'd think.

But Jen, she never exactly bought off on this line of thinking. She said men are foolish when it comes to their own death. Maybe we are. Anyway, there was no changing her mind, and that's one of the things I think about when I'm out in the barn, working at Taverner's bench and hammering Taverner's nails.

That, and how I wish I hadn't worked late in the butcher shop that Tuesday.

How she went ahead and ate supper without me.

How stupid it was of us not to double-check the seal on that one jar of his green beans.

Botulism, the doctors said.

Wigwam

Raymond Johnson's shoes look like hell. He knows it and prefers it that way. That's how badly he wants simply to blend in, to not stand out. Wear broken-down, brown lace-ups, he figures, and maybe people will start leaving him alone.

It's not just that they are large, which at size 16 they certainly are. It's more that they are sad shoes that have all the curb appeal of the run-down properties he shows as a rural real estate man. They are tired shoes that look as weary of their circumstance as the man wearing them. Yet man and shoes seem oddly at peace. A man who's long since run out of clever responses to tedious questions about how the weather is up there, put to him by shameless strangers in the mall who gawk at the amazing distance between his shoes and his head. The mall where it's not unusual to see seven-foot-tall Raymond with his short, intense-looking wife and their awkward daughter, moving among the shoppers in a practiced family formation, ignoring the stares, often holding hands.

It's also not unusual to see Raymond struggling in and out of his brown Toyota four-door at places like the post office. And the Texaco station. And the True Value. And on Sundays, at The Pancake House. But the most likely place to find Raymond Johnson, assuming anyone would ever go looking for him at all any more, is at athletic events at the small, parochial high school where he sends his daughter. In the fall it's volleyball. And then it's basketball.

He's impossible to miss in the bleachers. Everybody is aware of Raymond. But nobody sits by him or talks to him, though a few still gossip about him. Who he used to be. What he used to do before he began carrying *For Sale* signs around in the trunk of the Toyota. They say his name out of earshot and in the name of entertainment, because it's fun to say.

Wigwam Johnson.

Sprawled in his normal position at the top of the bleachers, the other thing that catches the meandering eye is the sharpness of his shins. Those shins are always showing, because Raymond's socks are always too short and his permanent press slacks are always hiked up a little too high. They are white and hairless shins. And there seems to be far too little mass or muscle to actually propel a man of Raymond's size. Which leads to more than a little speculation about how a man of so little bulk ever managed a career in professional basketball.

Most of the regulars in the high school gymnasium know how Raymond came by his name. He's long been part of Oregon sports lore. But it wasn't until he was drafted by the Baltimore Bullets that Wigwam Johnson became a household name across America. And it wasn't because of his skill or ability. But rather, it was because of a particularly caustic television sportscaster who delighted in pointing out that the coolest nickname in the Bullets' locker room belonged to a dime-a-dozen backup.

Nobody considered Raymond much of a prospect when he entered the NBA draft. But he was as tall as they came, so he qualified as a "project" center. A player of uncertain value who might develop, given the right coach, the right team, and enough time. His success in college mattered little.

Raymond's draft day jitters were more like spasms. He sat on his parents navy blue sofa, wearing his Linfield College sweatshirt and gym shorts, gripping and releasing his lean white thighs just above his bony knees, needing to pee but fearful of leaving the living room and missing the call, falsely believing that failure to answer the phone in person would result in his automatic disqualification.

Beyond the perimeter of the official waiting room, Raymond's well-wishers crowded in. The kitchen was chaos. The front porch looked like a church potluck. The backyard was awash in squinty-eyed working men and kinetic kids. Half the town of Mill City was there to experience the heady feeling of having one of their own make it big. To celebrate the boy who grew quickly and grew a lot, and who came to be named after the rusty wood debris burners that stand tall over the lumber mills that surround the town. Wigwam was a landmark as well.

Notably absent from the Johnson house was Tink Anderson, Raymond's college coach and mentor. By all accounts, the man struggled to accept that the only quality player he'd ever recruited couldn't stay in college forever. Which left him in no mood for celebrating. And which prompted him to spend draft day driving alone in his pick-up on mountain logging roads, smoking Raleigh Filters and trying to count the number of times he'd slapped Wigwam on his skinny butt in acknowledgement of a job well done. Tink kept losing count.

College was a high point for Raymond as well. It was the time when nearly everything went right for him. Professors went easy on him. Pretty girls said "hello" to him. High-paying summer jobs were thrown at him. And all he had to do was play in a game where a good many of his opponents were only tall enough to look straight into Raymond's belly.

On the rare occasion of something going wrong at Linfield, he came out of it okay. That's what happened when Raymond took a date to see Paul Revere and the Raiders one late September afternoon at the football stadium. They were seated about mid-way up in the old covered bleachers, and surrounded by other students. The music was good and the autumn air was sweet with the scent of burning leaves somewhere near campus. They couldn't really talk because the concert was too loud. Yet Raymond felt the need to let his date know how special she was to him that afternoon, how glad he was to be there with her. So in a move far less developed than his hook shot, he reached his right arm around behind his petite date, placed his hand gently but strongly on her waist, and pulled her into him. And all the while, Raymond kept his eyes on the band members and their white leotards, trying to be nonchalant and feeling somewhat disappointed that his date didn't have a more definite waistline.

This gesture would have worked fine if not for his long arms. But as it was, he'd reached well beyond the two seats where this date took place. He'd also reached beyond the space that separated them from the next couple down. Raymond had reached clear to the opposite side of the adjacent undergraduate. And the slight, young man protested loudly as he found himself being dislodged from his girlfriend and pulled snugly into the side of a co-ed he did not know.

In a life filled with awkward moments, this one nudged the top of Raymond's list. But there was an upside. Because as Raymond released his prey in a convulsion of embarrassment, and as Mark Lindsay sang loudly about how kicks just keep getting harder to find, Raymond locked onto the intense eyes of the girl whose boyfriend had suddenly levitated away. And there was something there. Both dates ended badly that day, but Raymond had found the short woman who would become his wife.

Serious dating wasn't really an option in high school. Raymond's life was filled with basketball, and being tall, and eating enough to power his growth spurts. He was the star of the Santiam Wolverines. Exactly the kind of high school basketball team you'd expect to see in a small, canyon community that's dominated by logging and family farms. Kids of all shapes and sizes and skill levels. This was Raymond's team, though. This was Raymond's town.

The Wolverines won their share of games during Raymond's reign. Even won their conference once. Winning can come in different forms, though. And for the people in and around canyon, it seemed to be enough to have everyone show up in support of Wigwam Johnson's Wolverines. Strapping lads in red and gray, each of whom had mastered the entry pass to their huge center, who then frustrated opposing teams by holding the ball near the rafters until he chose to flick it into the basket. Raymond was humble about all of this, his dominance due to height. Because as his mother's mother pointed out to him repeatedly, Raymond had nothing to do with the fact that he was big. That was his parents' doing. He was merely the beneficiary.

"The manifestation of recessive tall genes that came together to create a boy in high-water pants," his grandmother would say with an eyebrow raised.

Raymond took his grandmother's wisdom to heart, and it helped him keep his head on straight when people gushed over him. And he loved his grandmother for reminding him of his own truth. And it was somehow fitting that she died on a game day in February of Raymond's junior year. He played anyway, of course. Played his heart out, as grief-stricken athletes sometimes do. In addition to scoring more first-half points than ever before, and grabbing more first-half rebounds than anyone in conference history, mighty Wigwam jumped higher than he had ever jumped before. He seemed not to touch the court. It seemed as though his white high-tops were squeaking on the air beneath him. Raymond was a spectacle. The spectators were buzzing over his performance. The gym was in a trance, as was Raymond. But when Wigwam hit the back of his neck on the bottom of the backboard, it was as if the hypnotist had snapped his fingers. The people of Mill City awoke from their basketball trance just in time to see their hero crumple to the floor. Coaches and players rushed to Raymond. The town doctor charged out from the bleachers, as did a scout from Linfield. They encircled him under the basket, creating a temporary wall of secrecy and concern. After several tense minutes, the circle helped Raymond to his feet, and then guided him toward the locker room. And then, before the start of the second half, the P.A. system announced that Raymond "Wigwam" Johnson had suffered an injury that would keep him out of the remainder of the game. The truth stayed behind the pale green locker room door; that Raymond's pain was much less physical than emotional, and that he spent a long time in the showers, naked and alone, crying himself clean, talking to his grandmother.

She was the fan who mattered most.

She was the one who treated Raymond special well before he was a basketball star. She was the one who spent time with him, and listened to him, even when he spouted nonsense. She was the one who let Raymond and his fifth grade buddies camp out one Saturday night in the far back corner of her sprawling pasture, affording them all the opportunity to feel like they were out there completely on their own, self-sufficient and in no need of supervision. She was also the one who had fresh, hot cookies waiting when rain ruined the adventure, and the boys straggled in out of the darkness all cold and wet, happy to follow her orders about shedding their muddy boots and wet coats, and about sitting down at her yellow kitchen table. And of course, she was the one who, without letting the other boys see, took Raymond gently by the left ear as he entered, giving him the same reassuring little tug that she'd been giving him since before he had memories.

It rained the day Raymond's parents brought him home from the hospital. He was the new infant son of a couple who never imagined pregnancy was possible. They'd already settled into their lives as childless people who worked more than most, and who were content to sit opposite one another at the dinner table, describing the details of their days. They'd accepted their lot. But Baby Raymond changed all that.

The name Raymond came from the new mother's family in Nebraska. From her grandfather. He was a skilled horse trainer who smoked unfiltered cigarettes and drank Kentucky straight bourbon every day of his 97 years. Raymond's parents figured their young son might someday draw inspiration from being named for a man who endured in spite of his self-imposed obstacles. They also figured the old man would never hold or even see his great grandson, because he feared oceans, and maintained that Oregon's proximity to the Pacific made that state entirely unacceptable for travel, let alone everyday life.

New life was a wonder to Raymond's parents. They took turns staring down at their son in his crib. Other times, they stood there together, holding on to each other in disbelief. They studied Raymond's features, trying to decide who was responsible for what.

"Look at that hair," said Raymond's mother.

"That's some head of hair," agreed her husband.

"I think it comes from your side, because it's all thick and curly, like your brother. And nobody in my family has hair like that."

"Yes, you're probably right."

"But those eyes....now that's my family all over the place. Our famous hazel eyes."

"Just like yours, hun. But what about that nose? Who's gonna take responsibility for that?"

"Well, it's a little soon to tell, isn't it? But it appears to have the makings of a fine Roman nose. Which, if it is, I'm afraid your clan will have to own up to that one, Mr. Johnson."

"I suppose," he said as he grinned downward at Raymond. "I suppose."

Raymond was not a big infant. The doctor said he was actually fairly average. But there was something about Baby Raymond that was clearly not average, and it fired the Johnsons' speculation about the future of their son.

"Lord, look at those feet!", said Raymond's mother.

"I know."

Raymond's little soul came into this world at Santiam Memorial Hospital in nearby Stayton just two days prior, at just past ten in the morning. His first breath brought with it a wholly new set of circumstances and conditions—replete with the sort of inexplicable instincts and inclinations that help make every human unique. Those in the delivery room could see nothing more than a newborn. To a person they were ill equipped to understand more. Or to see more.

What they witnessed, however, was the return to earth of a soul who had been here many times before, and who had been sent back once again to continue with lessons that remained unlearned. That soul was at home most recently in the person of short man who sold shoes for a living in Chagrin Falls, Ohio, and who awoke most mornings with a list of worries among his first thoughts. A man who lived longer than he ever wanted, and who experienced more loss than he ever imagined possible. A man whose lifelong desire was simply to be tall, and then to be noticed, by anyone. Because being invisible felt like hell.

Suggested Questions for Book Clubs

Complicated relationships are rampant in these stories. Which relationships resonated with you? And why?

Can you point to aspects of these stories that satisfied an expectation you had as a reader?

Which characters did you care about most? (Did you recognize anyone you know personally among the characters in these stories?)

In which stories do you see the clearest influence of the natural world?

Which story or plot device caught you off guard?

If you could rewrite the ending of a story, which one and why?

Pretend for a moment that all of the female characters came together to discuss this book. What might they have to say about how the author portrayed them?

Saying thanks in person may not always carry adequate weight, or even be practicable. But when you offer thanks in ink, it can be worth far more than the paper it's printed on. Or so I hope.

And with that caveat, my heartfelt thanks go first to Gayle Hannahs, who as my official first reader helped me to see storytelling opportunities and issues that I could not. My life would simply be less without her wisdom, candor, and love.

Thank you to Mike and Kandee McClain, my beta readers. Their passion for the written word combined with their instincts as educators to yield key insights that helped this book ripen properly. Thanks as well to Erica Witbeck for her discerning notes. Hats off to Bryan Tomasovich, whose editorial prowess helped me groom this work into its final form. Paramount among his reminders to me was the value of trusting the reader. Bryan also did a crackerjack job of interior page layout. Likewise, Heather John earned my appreciation for bringing the cover design to graphic fruition—taking full advantage of the gossamer photo by Alden Rodgers, and the original poster concept created years ago by acclaimed art director Andrew Reed when he and I were creative collaborators in the world of advertising. Also, here's a shout-out to illustrator Kurt Hollomon, yet another talented friend from back in the day, for his renderings of those darn crows.

Finally, special thanks go to the people of the North Santiam Canyon: a few of them contributed knowingly to these stories, but many more contributed in ways they'll never know.

About the Author

Dan T. Cox was born in Corvallis, Oregon in 1953. He grew up in Oregon's North Santiam Canyon, earned a journalism degree from the University of Oregon, became part of Portland's advertising creative community, and now lives in Ridgefield, Washington. His short fiction has appeared in literary journals such as *Weber Studies* and *Skyline*. His first book of short stories was titled *A Bigger Piece of Blue/stories*. *The Canyon Cuts Both Ways/hidden stories* is his second book.